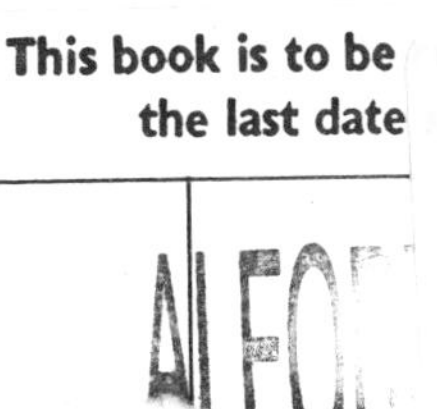

"This wonderfully original debut novel is an engaging read. It is a particularly moving and unusual story of suspense and intrigue with well drawn out characters with whom readers will be able to empathize. The scientific nature of the story and the ethical questions it raises will challenge readers' opinions and encourage discussion."
Caroline Gibson, *Principal Teacher and Education Development Officer*

"This is an original idea, written with a light and entertaining touch...but, my goodness, it's gripping!"
Gabrielle Rollinson, *Continuing Education, University of Liverpool*

D.M. Simons

Front cover photograph by Kevin P.G. Wong

Matador
5 Weir Road
Kibworth Beauchamp
Leicester LE8 0LQ, UK
Tel: (+44) 116 279 2299
Fax: (+44) 116 279 2277
Email: books@troubador.co.uk
Web: www.troubador.co.uk/matador

ISBN 978 1848766 976

British Library Cataloguing in Publication Data.
A catalogue record for this book is available from the British Library.

Printed and bound in the UK by TJ International, Padstow, Cornwall

Typeset in 11pt Book Antiqua by Troubador Publishing Ltd, Leicester, UK

Matador is an imprint of Troubador Publishing Ltd

For my father, Andrew G. Reid and in memory of my mother, Marion O. Reid, and for my uncle, Alwyn H.G. Jones who has been like a second father to us.

ACKNOWLEDGEMENTS

I am grateful to my sister, Alison Robertson, who cast some of her own ideas, like diamonds, throughout the text during early proof reads. Something else that I will always treasure is the unbounded enthusiasm for my story expressed by my nephew, Craig. My own children, Kyle, Kevin, James and Hannah, deserve no less thanks, for it is they who made sure that my dialogue kept within the realms of their own generation. I would like to give a special thank you to my friends, Julie and Caitlin Taylor, Gordon D. Brown, Stephen, Olivia, William and Isobel Passey and fellow author, Rebecca Morton, who read *Keep Her Safe* and offered me valuable feedback. Also, I am grateful to Laura Martin and her Primary 6 Class for reading my drafts of Chapters 1 & 2 and encouraging me to continue. I would also like to thank Amanda Duncan for helping with the legal terminology. Not least for my husband, Simon, an enormous thank you for tolerating the many pets that I need to surround me when I write.

PROLOGUE

One glimpse of him through her spy hole and she knew he'd need only one or two kicks to break down her thin, hollow door. This was all that separated her from certain danger. Now shaking, her arthritic fingers fumbled to slide the security chain in place.

'Open up, old woman, I've come about your brother.' The slick voice oozed through the wood.

'I don't have any brothers,' she lied, her heart quickening.

'I'm a friend of his, Miss Ivanhoe.' But she didn't believe him. Her brother had warned her that one day a stranger might come looking for him. They'd use her to find him – to find the chuman.

'Please leave.' She put her hand to her chest. What was it her brother had told her to do? It had been over four years now. She'd almost forgotten there was any danger at all. Her chest was tightening – it was getting harder to breathe. She backed away from the door.

'Let me in, I've something to tell you.'

A card appeared in between the door and its frame. It jiggled up and down. She glanced towards her living room where her phone lay, too far away. Suddenly, the door popped free of the lock and crashed the chain. A massive pair of wire cutters snapped the chain and the door flung open.

She stepped back, her breath coming in short gasps. A dark haired man filled the frame. He lurched forwards and kick-slammed the door. The sound vibrated in her bones. He stepped closer, his head blocking the ceiling light which shone around him and she couldn't see his face properly.

'Have you any tea on the brew? Let's go look, shall we?' he asked. Confused, Miss Ivanhoe stumbled.

He sat at her kitchen table and drummed his gloved fingers on the polished wood. Gloves in summer? She knew he would leave no trace of his visit. The tremor in her hands grew and spread along her arms to her shoulders.

When's he going to ask me about little…? She glanced at the cabinet – glad she'd locked away the photos. Her throat was now so tight, she felt suffocated.

'I'm waiting.'

She picked up the teapot and splashed tea into the cup and saucer. She passed it across to him, the cup rattling in the saucer like a skeleton in a breeze.

The man's Adam's apple bounced as he gulped. Smash. Tinkle. The teacup imploded under the crushing pressure of his fist.

Miss Ivanhoe jerked. Her ears rang.

'Sometimes I forget the strength of my own hands.' He grinned lopsidedly. 'As a child, I killed a rat with them.' He exposed his wrist, revealing a pair of scars – from the rat's bite, she guessed. 'That was the beginning of my career as the *Inflictor*.'

Miss Ivanhoe steadied herself against the work surface, urging herself not to faint.

'I think you were expecting someone like me, eventually. The chuman, Miss Ivanhoe, where is it? My clients know that your brother faked its death four years ago, stole it and fled. Don't bother denying it.' His icy eyes chilled the room.

A wave of love for those she cared for gave her strength. 'Your clients, whoever they are, are evil.'

The Inflictor snorted, and a deep scar pulled his face into a hideous contortion.

'I'll never tell you,' she said, her heart pounding.

He stood, knocked the chair over and in one stride stood before her. Unsteady, she stepped backwards, her ears singing. She almost hoped she'd die of a heart attack before he beat the information out of her.

His brows came together, blackening his eyes. 'Now, I *will* have that address.'

'You're going to kill me anyway. I'm just like that rat to you.'

As he moved still closer, a multitude of bursting bubbles filled her vision.

* * *

Minutes later, the Inflictor sat in his black Maserati, sealed from the respectable neighbourhood outside. He whipped off the wig and typed an address into a satellite navigation device. Such an easy job for the money he was charging. Just before starting the car, he caught sight of his reflection in the rear view mirror. His left eye had swivelled upwards - again. With one finger he adjusted it forwards. Then, spotting some blood spray on his cheek, he used his sleeve to wipe it.

CHAPTER 1

The incessant roar of rushing water from the nearby stream was keeping Nikki awake. Inside her sleeping bag she squeezed her cuddly elephant against her chest and wished she wasn't alone. It had been so much more fun the last time she'd camped; she smiled, remembering the pillow fight with her dad. *But that can never happen again and it's all my fault.* She wriggled onto her back and a tear trickled into her ear. She blinked and watched the shadows of leaves silently dancing over her tent in the moonlight.

Outside, inches from her face, something brushed against the flimsy tent wall. She tensed and listened. Something sniffed – rapidly and deeply. Her heart quickened and her fists clutched the sleeping bag to her chin. That was no hedgehog – it was much bigger. She thought of the huge red-eyed werewolves in the book that lay beside her. Claws scraped against the backpack that she'd left out there. It had to be something like a fox looking for food. A shadow glided across the tent – was there a second one? She tried to breathe silently so that they, whatever they were, wouldn't hear, and she anchored her heels to drag herself further away.

A click sounded, followed by a second click, then a

cord pulled. That's no animal, she thought, it must be Nathan and Lyle raiding for a midnight feast. She checked her watch by the feeble torchlight – after two a.m. She eased herself out of her sleeping bag. Now it sounded like someone was rummaging in the pack. She already wore her fleecy over her pyjamas and now shoved her feet into trainers. She unzipped the tent slowly, hoping it wouldn't be heard. Opposite, the boys' tent sagged, catching soft light from the full moon that hung in the blue-grey summer night sky. But their door remained zipped up and no sound came from within. She crawled part way out and flashed her torch around her own tent, finding no sign of anyone or any animal, only the backpack lying opened on its side, spilling a couple of tins and a jar of sauce.

She gasped – something moved behind the tent. She shifted the beam and it swept over a hump – something was crouching. It skittered off into the darkness, sprinkling her pyjamas with grit. It was small and ran on all fours at first but soon rose up, speeding on two legs. What *was* that? Heart thudding and keeping her beam on the fleeing creature, she stepped out to follow, but her foot caught a tent rope. The boys' tent shuddered and the ground seemed to come up to smack her, knocking the wind from her chest. Small stones pressed into her cheek and her long brown waves covered her face. She spat out dirt and instinctively touched her hair – still in place. A few metres away, the creature splashed across the stream. Dare she follow it?

'What are you doing?' her cousin Nathan's sleepy voice came from his tent.

'Something's just raided our food bag.' She reached for her fallen torch. 'I'm following it before it gets too far.' Its shape and size reminded her of the Tasmanian devil in the cartoon. Was it as fierce as that? Could she really follow it alone? 'Coming?' she asked hopefully.

'It'll be a fox. Just leave it,' Nathan said, sounding irritated. 'Go back to sleep.' She heard him swishing around in his nylon sleeping bag.

'A fox couldn't undo the straps on the bag, could it?' And she headed for the stream, flashing torchlight into every bush. 'And it ran on two legs.'

The boys' tent unzipped. 'Could've been a druggie looking for something to steal,' Nathan called after her.

'No. It definitely wasn't human. But it was dressed, so it wasn't an animal either.' She'd never catch up with it now; never find out what it was.

'Wait,' said Nathan, putting on his trainers. 'I'm awake now - might as well come.'

'Not animal. Not human. Maybe it's a tree-spirit,' said Lyle, sounding amused and poking his head out from behind Nathan. 'My gran says that spirits of the dead live in trees, so maybe - '

'Will you shut up about tree-spirits,' said Nikki, preferring to think of her dad in heaven and not up a tree. 'I know it sounds stupid, but it looked like a leprechaun, a little person of some kind - if they existed.'

'That's ridiculous,' said Nathan with a laugh.

'Hurry up or we'll be too late to find anything,' she moaned, and continued towards the stream.

'Look, Chieftain's not bothered,' Nathan pointed out, draping his sleepy Siamese cat around his shoulders as he caught up with her. 'He would've freaked if anything was wrong.'

A bush rustled and Chieftain hissed, springing off Nathan's shoulder. He stood on tiptoe, arching his back and staring at the bush.

'You spoke too soon, Nathan,' Nikki whispered, goose bumps tickling over her skin. 'There must be another one.'

'What's up, Chief?' asked Nathan, stroking the cat's spine, trying to flatten the levitating fur. But Chieftain growled again and slunk back to the tent.

'Can you see anything?' Nikki asked.

From within the undergrowth, leaves rustled under rapidly moving feet. Nikki backed away. Something big and black barrelled out and came to a sudden stop. It was a second before Nikki's mind registered it to be a Labrador. It stared at her with eyes reflecting gold in her torchlight and from his mouth a packet spilled biscuits – theirs. Tail wagging, he swaggered towards her, trailing broken digestives.

'Hey, Nikki,' said Lyle, joining them. 'There's your leprechaun.'

'It's nothing like it,' she replied, glancing enviously at his more powerful torch. 'Besides, it's already crossed the stream.'

'Shush,' warned Nathan. 'You'll wake the other campers.'

The Lab sniffed Nikki's hand. 'There's no collar. I suppose he must've come from our campground.' She prised the packet from his mouth and a swinging string of drool glued itself to her wrist. Wrinkling her nose, she wiped it on her pyjamas.

'Seriously, though, it's dark – the mind can play tricks,' said Lyle.

'You really think a dog could undo our bag?' she retorted. 'And look there, it dropped our apples right by the stream. And over there, that's our Cheerios box.' She sat the saliva-covered packet with the apples. The dog joined her, sniffed the air and splashed away across the stream towards the woods.

'The dog took food too, so he must've seen the creature. Maybe he can smell it, maybe he knows where it is,' she said, and tried to spot the driest stones to step on. As if wanting her to follow, the dog sat watching from the opposite bank.

'Okay, let's go over the river and into the land of make believe,' teased her cousin.

'Shut up,' she replied. The moonlight and shadows played tricks with the wet stones. Her eyes were confused and just as she reached the other side, she slipped off of a wet rock, soaking her foot.

Nathan laughed. 'Alright, alright. Just let me get Chieftain. There's no way I'm leaving him behind in case he's stolen. He's worth over three hundred quid.'

But what chance did she have now of finding the creature? Unless the dog actually did know where it was. She touched his silky head and, not waiting for the boys, followed him upstream on the grassy path. She noticed his limp – must be old, she thought, but I still feel safer with him.

The boys came up behind her and after only a few minutes, Nathan muttered, 'This is pointless, let's go back.' Wondering if she really had imagined such a creature, Nikki was about to give up too when the dog turned off the path. He trotted stiffly towards a small hillock that had a tumbledown structure at the top. Near the foot of the hill, the Lab stopped and lay down in front of a large elongated grass-covered mound. It appeared to have a dark opening. Did the creature live in there?

'That's an Earth House,' said Lyle, coming up beside her. 'I've been in one before, on a school trip. They're really old – Iron Age or something.'

'Can I borrow your torch?' Nikki asked him.

From a few feet away she shone it at the stone framed entrance. Camouflaged with moss and sprouting ferns, it blended in with the landscape but the heavy stone lintel over the entrance was highlighted with a large splash of bluish-white lichen. She crouched to aim the beam inside, like a vet shining a light into the throat of a gigantic snake. How far back did it go? Judging by the grassy mound it made on the surface, it could be fifteen or more metres.

'You can go inside,' said Lyle. 'It was probably used for storing food.'

'Couldn't it be a burial chamber?' Nathan asked. 'Maybe it still has bones in it. That'd be cool.'

'Dunno. Go on in, Nikki, and see if your creature's there,' Lyle urged. 'It's perfectly safe, otherwise it'd be blocked off.'

Nikki sighed. Spiders would be just as bad as skulls, but as for an unknown wild creature… Her heart thudded – she could see its beating action on her fleecy and folded her arms to hide it.

'She's too chicken to go in there at night,' said Nathan.

Why did he always have to make fun of her in front of his friends? Why did he have to bring Lyle? How could she be herself with a stranger around? This camping trip was supposed to do her good, her mum had said. Well, not so far. She sighed. 'Of course I can do it, but you two should come in and see too.'

'It's your creature, but we'll come if you're too scared…' said her cousin, grinning, no doubt in anticipation of her failure. She wanted to turn and walk away, to pretend she wasn't bothered, but there was no way out. If she didn't show them she could do it, Nathan would keep reminding her forever. Trying to sound casual, she said, 'No problem.' Her gaze dropped to the huge puddle that lay in the entrance, like a pool of saliva in the snake's mouth. Stones protruded like teeth from the earth around it. She reached inwards to light up the ceiling, aware her arm was shaking.

'How about letting Chieftain go first, he's a cat and actually likes exploring that sort of place,' she suggested.

'I don't want him attacked by your weird creature,' Nathan replied.

What about me? she thought. 'But you said he'd freak if anything was wrong.'

'True. Hold the dog.'

Nikki grabbed a handful of loose skin at the back of the Lab's neck while Nathan set his cat down in front of the Earth House entrance. The cat twitched his ruffled fur and looked around before sniffing at the puddle and stepping around it and into the blackness.

'You'll not be alone now,' said her cousin, but Nikki hardly heard him. She'd noticed a partially submerged banana skin in the puddle.

'That probably came from our bunch,' she said, using her foot to drag it out. This must mean that she hadn't imagined the creature and that it really could be in there.

She ducked under the low lintel and moved part way inside. The roughly cut stones of the ceiling and walls had been fitted together so skilfully, but after thousands of years, could she really trust them not to cave in on her? She could go just a little further in and still be able to escape quickly. The torch first illuminated Chieftain's backside and then she shone it around the stone-lined passage. It was over a metre in diameter and height, but she could imagine it contracting in on her, swallowing her into the bowels of the earth. What if a spider dropped onto her neck? She pictured its shining black eye clusters and hairy legs creeping silently, and her breathing became faster.

The torch light could just pick out what she thought must be the back wall, maybe fifteen or even twenty metres in. Gaps along either side of the passage looked like chambers - full of skulls and bones, no doubt. She counted six of them. Crouching, she shuffled past the puddle, as if it were a pool of acid. Still no sound from inside. Behind her, the boys were talking as if they'd forgotten all about her. Maybe she could still go back?

Nathan shouted, 'Haven't you seen your creature yet?' She could hear them laughing now and felt a wave of rage sweep through her. She inched along the dirt floor, deeper into the passageway, shining the light to her left into the first chamber, a circular room of about two metres in diameter. No skulls, thankfully. She moved along to the second chamber, then the third. She was now more than halfway in. Not being able to stand up would make it harder to run. She aimed the light into the fourth chamber. Someone had stuck some wild flowers, now dead, and a candle on a jutting out stone. Modern day Druids, she guessed, hoping there weren't any in there. The torch was becoming slippery in her sweating hand.

Something brushed past her leg; she shrieked and dropped the torch, which went out. Panicking, she grappled around with both hands, getting dirt under her nails and hoping that she wouldn't touch the creature. At last her hand clamped around the plastic handle. She shook it, and the torch's loose battery slid back into place and immediately it lit up. Gulping air, she swept the beam up and down the stone passage. What was in there with her?

The only sign of life was Chieftain casually walking back towards the moonlit opening. Nikki brought her free hand to her throat and slowly exhaled. He's right, she thought, time to leave.

She was about to move when a shiver went down her neck – she felt sure that she was being watched, and it obviously wasn't Chieftain. She turned the beam behind her – just stone walls. Sucking in air, she flashed the torch all around her. Something white stood out in the darkness: a skull with huge curved horns, which made her think of devil worship. She hadn't seen it before. Where was she – had she got to the fifth chamber? Then there was just one more to check. If the creature was in the Earth House, it had to be in that one.

She swallowed. I'm ready, she tried to assure herself. She breathed out and edged up to view chamber number six. A shuffling noise came from within it. Blood pulsed loudly in her ears and, panting, she held the torch towards the little room, but wasn't close enough to see inside. Something coughed. Her heart pounded, this must be it – the creature. She was too far in to call the guys and didn't want to shout and spur the creature into attack. Not wanting to expose her back, she leant against the wall and inched sideways towards the chamber. Something grunted. Gasping, she swung the torch straight into the chamber.

Huge white teeth gleamed in a broad mouth with the lips peeled back. Black eyes glinted on either side of nostrils lifted in a grimace. Nikki screamed – the sound was stifled, trapped with her in the musty air and locked under several feet of stone and earth. She felt buried alive. Her mouth dried, her heart tumbled. The creature's cavernous mouth opened and let out a piercing, inhuman scream. Nikki fell back against the cold wall, holding her hands and torch to protect her face. This thing was real – alive. Desperate to get out, she pushed away from the wall and crawled towards the dawn light, tearing holes in her thin pyjamas and almost smashing Lyle's torch. The dog shot in towards her, barking, and almost cut off her only escape. But she shoved past him and jumped up to dive under the lintel.

Her forehead struck stone and pain exploded in her

head. She fell sideways into the shallow pool of muddy water. She felt herself sinking into a deep sea, swirling around and around, the darkness sucking her down until she forgot where she was and her mind turned black.

CHAPTER 2

Nikki came to, aware of being scraped along the ground with dirt and stones gathering under her clothes. She was soaked and cold. Beneath her, hard ground turned to soft grass and she was dragged for several more feet before being flipped onto her back. She looked up into a boy's face framed by shaggy brown hair. His shirt, splashed with muddy water, sagged towards her. A second face appeared – a Chinese boy. Behind them was a deep blue sky with fading stars. After a couple of seconds delay her memory kicked in – Nathan and his friend Lyle Cheung. I'm still alive, the creature didn't even touch me, she thought.

'Are you alright?' asked her cousin. 'Your head's bleeding.'

Remembering her hair, she reached for it and touched around her head – still in place, just wet and muddy. She felt the sticky blood on her forehead. Then the pain hammered and she felt dizzy. I must look terrible, she thought, wishing Lyle wasn't there. The dog sniffed her neck and put a tongue out to lick her. She leaned away, her head spinning.

'I'm fine,' she said, wondering if she'd actually cracked her skull. 'Just get him away from me.'

'What happened?' asked Lyle.

'The creature *is* in there, it's… it's really weird,' she stammered. She sat up and stared towards the entrance, where the darkness merged with the black dog that now lay there as if guarding his lair. 'It's like nothing you've ever seen before.'

'It still could've been a fox,' suggested Lyle.

'No, it's like I already told you…' she was panting now. 'It was like a goblin or a leprechaun. That's the only way I can describe it.'

Nathan laughed and said, 'She's hallucinating – she's had a bump on the head.'

'It's okay, it *was* dark in there,' said Lyle, sounding kind.

'Chieftain's not freaked so it couldn't have been even as scary as a dog to him,' said Nathan.

She looked at his Siamese cat, now perched on the low mound of the Earth House, well back from the dog. Had he actually seen the creature? Maybe it was supernatural and only appeared once she was alone or maybe it was the ghost of a deformed child buried there long ago. That was ridiculous, of course, but goose bumps still prickled on the back of her neck.

'Come on, Nathan. Let's check it out,' said Lyle. 'How big was this thing, Nikki?'

'I don't know, it looked big in there, but quite small at the campsite. It had a huge mouth and teeth and it screamed at me.'

'I only heard *you* scream,' said Nathan, heading to the dark entrance with Lyle.

Nikki glared after him.

Nathan laughed. 'She thinks she saw a goblin.'

She shot back, 'It *was* real. You never believe anything I say.' It sounded childish – but why couldn't Nathan ever take her seriously?

'Ahh!' yelled Nathan.

Nikki's heart pumped faster and she looked up to see both boys jump backwards as if avoiding waves at the shore. It had to be the creature. She stood up, but staggered, her vision misting for a second. Puddle water splashed up in jets and a small human-like creature burst from the darkness with eyes shining in the moonlight. She could hear rapid breathing hissing through its gleaming teeth. It leapt over the dog and shot between the boys. Taking a turn to avoid Nikki, it looked straight into her eyes and sped off. It ran upright on disproportionately short legs and was dressed in dark coloured leggings and a grey hoody. As it ran, the hood slipped off revealing dark, straggly, shoulder length hair. The dog got up, tail wagging, and trotted after it.

'What the bloody hell was that?' asked Lyle.

'Beats me, hurry, let's follow it,' said Nathan. 'Nikki, watch Chieftain.'

Still sitting in the grass, Nikki shouted, 'I told you.' But they ignored her. She stared after the creature. It ran across the pasture, scattering a group of sheep, and headed towards the heather-covered hillock with a roofless, crumbling stone structure silhouetted against the lightening sky.

How could this be real? She blinked hard. She'd just been face to face with a creature that could not exist – at least not since before the Stone Age. She touched the blood on her forehead. Maybe she was actually unconscious and this was all a dream.

But there it was running, and faster than she would've thought possible for its size, especially now it was going up the steep hill. But the boys were gaining on it. Lyle paused to grab a stick from the ground. The creature, followed by the dog, slipped under the archway of what was left of an entrance to the ancient building and disappeared from sight. The boys weren't far behind.

Nikki glanced back at the Earth House entrance and decided she'd rather be away from it in case any more creatures came out. Her head throbbed when she got up and climbed onto the mound to get Chieftain. He blinked at her and, as always, he seemed to turn into a heavy rag when she scooped him up. It was as if he was too lazy to use any muscles at all. He must have noticed the creature in the chamber, but acted as if nothing was amiss. She hung him around her neck, in the way that Nathan usually carried him.

'You're not a normal cat, Chieftain,' she told him, holding both pairs of paws that hung over her shoulders. She headed across the pasture and found a grassy path that wound between clumps of heather towards the top of the hillock.

'I think we've lost it,' said Nathan, standing on the low wall of the circular structure.

'Watch out for all the sheep uh, you know what,' warned Lyle, joining his friend. Nikki glanced down. It was getting quite light now and she could see what he meant.

At last she reached the ancient building and

Chieftain sprang onto the arch when she stooped to enter. The action made her woozy and she rubbed the scratch Chieftain had just left on her neck. Not feeling up to climbing the walls, she stepped carefully among the many fallen blocks of stone that lay in the centre of the structure, which stretched to about eight metres in diameter. Over the far wall, she could see distant mountains, dark against the dawn. Skye was such a tranquil island. What was this strange beast that lived out here underground? Had she just discovered a new species? Where was it now? Nothing ran out from the stones as she picked about them and she couldn't see anywhere for it to hide.

'Could there be another underground chamber here?' asked Nathan.

'No, this isn't an Earth House. Isn't it one of those Iron Age round houses?' she asked.

'Yeah, it's called a Broch,' called Lyle over his shoulder.

'Looks like a pile of old rocks to me,' said Nathan.

'Well, where could it be...' Nikki began, and felt the Lab's thick tail beating against her legs. His rear was sticking out of a tiny stone room built into the wall.

Her heart thudded. Could the creature be hiding there? She did want a good look at it, but what if it attacked them? She shoved the dog to the side and squatted to peer in – not too close, though. She shone her own weak torch in but could only see a boulder and a few fallen stones. The domed ceiling was just over a metre above the earth floor. Light spilled through a hole where it'd caved in. The dog was sniffing at the boulder and whining, but she couldn't see any creature.

'Come on, boy,' she called, but she couldn't distract him.

'Is it under there?' asked Nathan, from the wall above her.

The boulder moved.

Nikki almost fell backwards, 'I... I think it is.'

Nathan and Lyle dropped down beside her. There wasn't much space for their feet among the stones.

'I'll check it out,' said Lyle, crouching to stare for a moment, then he reached in with his stick. Nikki held her breath. He gave the grey boulder a prod. It squealed.

'It's an animal,' he said, sounding excited. 'It must be the one.' He prodded it again. Again, it squealed and squirmed.

'Careful, Lyle, you're provoking it,' warned Nikki, remembering that a cornered animal could be really dangerous.

Behind them, the dog levelled his head at Lyle and barked.

'Hey, Lyle, you'd better stop,' said Nikki.

But he poked it again. 'I'm not doing it hard, I just want to see it properly.'

In the darkest corner, the mound whimpered and contracted into an even smaller ball.

'Lyle, stop it,' said Nikki. 'It's a living thing.' She didn't want to hear that horrible scream again, nor see its teeth.

The creature gave a muffled cry.

Another jab. 'I just want it to open up.'

'Lyle, stop,' Nikki shouted.

The dog went on barking.

The mound rocked to and fro, expanding and contracting as it breathed. They all fell silent and backed away. Nikki knew that it must be very angry. Something was going to happen. Her fingers tightened around Nathan's T-shirt sleeve.

Suddenly, the creature-ball seemed to explode, screeching and spinning round to stand upright, facing them with fists swinging as low as its knees. It swayed, hissing through its teeth. Pale light through the hole in the ceiling cast shadows from its heavy brow down its smudged face, from which hair sprouted as a fuzzy frame. The snarl that began on one side of its mouth spread to include the other and the sound became a throaty roar.

CHAPTER 3

Beings like this can't exist, Nikki thought. Keeping her torch aimed on the creature, she stepped back and staggered over a stone. Lyle caught her arm and pulled her up.

'I'm fine,' she muttered, wriggling her arm free but keeping her eyes on the creature.

Its mouth opened wider and wider, while the roar rose in pitch to a piercing scream. She could see the wobbly thing vibrating and glinting at the opening of its throat. She covered her ears and the hair on her arms and neck stood on end.

The dog manoeuvred himself between them and the creature.

'Shut up with the barking,' Lyle shouted at him.

The creature looked at Lyle and snapped its teeth shut, but left the thin lips lifted, showing its fangs.

Nikki's ears were still ringing with the scream. She glanced at the Lab. 'He's barking at us – not the creature. It's as if he's protecting it.'

The creature's eyes screwed up and tears leaked from the corners and tracked down its dirty cheeks. It appeared almost child-like. The eyes then became wide and very human, and the gaze that met Nikki's held terror.

'Only humans can cry,' she whispered. 'I think it was bluffing – it's actually really scared.' They'd trapped it there in that tiny room.

The creature dropped down to a crouch again and wrapped long arms over its head, shielding itself from their stares. It squeezed its head tighter, pulling itself back into a ball.

'Do you think there's a whole family of them?' she asked. 'Or is she someone's kid with some kind of weird syndrome?'

'It must have parents, weird or not,' said Lyle.

'Yeah, even you have parents,' Nathan teased.

'Someone dressed her,' Nikki observed.

'*Her*?' Lyle raised an eyebrow.

'There are flowers on the trousers.' She pointed to the machine embroidered spray of red flowers on the leggings near an exposed bit of ankle.

'Man, look at those big hairy hobbit's feet,' Nathan exclaimed.

'Yeah, it looks like Gollum,' said Lyle.

Nikki stared at the creature's feet and didn't think that any shoes could fit with such a thumb-like big toe.

'Seriously, it must be some kind of genetically mutated freak,' Lyle continued.

There was that word Nikki hated to hear. Freak. How many times had she been called that? She didn't think she could bear it if he called her that. She shook her head to clear the memories. 'But where did she come from? There's no one around, so maybe she's lost. Let's try asking her.' She felt uncomfortable with the quivering, whimpering heap, buried under its own arms. Tentatively, she reached out her hand but the dog growled a warning.

The creature jumped up, thrust her arms up through the hole in the ceiling and hauled herself through. She spun round and shot off along the Broch wall and jumped down out of sight.

Nikki and the others rushed to the wall and saw her fleeing down the far side of the hillock. The creature looked tiny, weaving her way among the bracken and heather. The dog bounded after her, his tongue flapping to one side of his mouth.

'Wait, wait!' shouted Nikki. 'We won't hurt you, we only want to help you.'

'I'll catch her. You get Chieftain,' Nathan yelled, climbing over the wall.

Nikki found the Siamese on a patch of soft grass padding the Broch wall. He looked up from licking between his spread open toes, obviously not bothered by the drama. She gathered him up and headed down the slope on legs that still felt weak.

The creature seemed to fly along on her short legs but Nathan was faster, sprinting with arms flailing about for balance as he swerved around heather. The gap closed between them and he reached out to catch hold of her arm. Immediately she swung it free but Nathan quickly caught her by the shoulders and turned her to face him. Nikki saw her bare her teeth again and heard a sound that was somewhere between a growl and whine.

Nathan let go. Lyle staggered towards them, stooping with his arms apart, ready to trap her. The creature looked from Nathan to Lyle and back again. The dog bounded between the boys and the creature, his tail wagging as if it were a game.

Nikki caught them up and handed Chieftain over to Nathan. The creature's eyes flashed to hers.

'It's alright. Are you lost? Can you understand us?' she asked softly. She stooped down to the creature's height, keeping a comfortable distance. The creature kept her gaze locked on Nikki and the rise and fall of her chest slowed. Nikki studied the little face with its broad set eyes, freckle-sprinkled nose and large sticking out ears. She was quite cute, now that she was calmer. The creature frowned and tilted her head. Her eyes became questioning, searching. Nikki felt exposed, naked. It felt as if the creature had just read her innermost thoughts and feelings. She felt the blood drain from her face. Did she see what only Nikki had seen after that accident? How it was her fault that her dad had died? Did she know about what happened to her hair? Surely it was impossible to read minds. It was bad enough that God could read her mind, if he existed. But this was no normal being. Nikki touched her hair and glanced at the guys, wondering if the creature was at least as intelligent as the rest of them.

The dog sat down beside the creature and without taking her eyes off Nikki and the others, the creature flung her arms around his neck.

Nikki sighed, glad that the creature's attention was taken away from her. She realised how cold and damp she felt and glanced over her shoulder towards the Broch.

'What do we do now? I kind of want to go back,' she said, looking at the creature who was now kissing the dog's floppy ears. 'Aw, look at that. Could it be *her* dog?' The creature nodded. 'Hey guys, did you see that? She nodded – that means she *can* understand us. Maybe she can talk too. Where are your mum and dad? Are they at the campground? Who looks after you?' But the creature just kept shaking her head. 'Did you run away?' This time the creature looked away, nodding slowly.

'Maybe it escaped from a circus,' suggested Lyle.

'I hope that's not true,' said Nikki. 'Anyway, on Skye? There's only a couple of small towns here.'

Nathan frowned. 'Why would she run away? Was someone mean to her?'

'Where d'you live?' asked Nikki, but the creature shook her head. 'Will you show us?' The creature only shook her head more vigorously. 'Can you talk?' The creature just blinked at them.

'*Are you human*?' Lyle muttered.

Nikki wondered the same thing, but only said, 'I wish she could tell us her name.'

'What do we do now?' asked Nathan.

'We can't just abandon her,' said Nikki.

'It's got nothing to do with us – we don't know anything about it,' said Lyle. 'It might have some strange disease that we could catch.'

'Not even an animal will run away from home without good reason,' Nikki pointed out. 'If we abandon her, she could die of starvation. Nathan, we could ask your mum.'

She turned to the creature, 'Would you like to come with us and have something to eat?' Nikki saw the creature grin for the first time and long cool fingers reached out to gather around her own, the sensation immediately reminding of her grandfather's leathery hands.

They turned and headed back through the scratchy heather and sheep towards the campground. The Lab walked at the creature's heel wherever there was enough space. Nikki wondered if he'd been trained to look after her, and if she actually did have a good home. She looked strange and her hair was a mess, but she wasn't ill or starved, and the clothes weren't bad – just dirty. She watched how the creature walked – upright. Only people walk upright, so she must be a child born with some sort of abnormality.

Nikki, lost in her own thoughts, was only vaguely aware of the boys still speculating together – where did the creature come from, what was she and what should they do with her?

Lyle caught up with her and asked, 'What do you reckon?' Before she could answer, the creature released her hand and bounded towards the tents.

'And by the way, guys, I'm still waiting for an apology for not believing me,' said Nikki.

'Yeah well, it's no goblin, is it?' said Nathan, laughing.

'And it's not scary at all,' added Lyle.

She let the boys walk ahead and stared after them, hating people who couldn't admit being wrong. They swaggered so confidently. Nathan looked so skinny, how could he be strong enough to have a black belt in Tae Kwon Do? Lyle was shorter, but definitely more robust.

Then she hurried past them to catch up with the creature who was now splashing across the stream that bounded the campground. It was now light enough for Nikki to easily avoid the rocks slick with slimy green algae. The birds were singing loudly but all the tents remained zipped up and the tables bare.

Nikki checked her watch. 'Hey guys, it's not even four a.m. so we'd better keep quiet.'

The creature found the second backpack storing their food, deftly undid the strap clips and loosened the cords. Like a toddler, she pulled everything out. Frowning, she examined and sniffed all of the packets.

'I'm just going to get changed,' said Nikki and then from her tent, continued, 'she seems very intelligent. I mean there doesn't seem to be much wrong with her brain.'

'Just her hairy hands and feet,' said Nathan.

'And her beard,' said Lyle, with a laugh.

'Guys, whatever it is, she can't help it. Anyway, we'll have to help her get back to – wherever.'

She touched her fingertips all around her head and brushed the dried mud and grass from her hair, wishing she'd remembered to bring a mirror. She'd have a shower later in Nathan's parents' caravan. She emerged in denim shorts and a clean fleecy. 'I need something for my head.'

'Oh, nasty,' said Nathan, and went to get the first aid kit. Lyle looked over and grinned. Nikki's mouth twitched in response. Had Nathan told him much about her? *Not everything,* she hoped.

When he returned, Nikki lowered her voice, 'You didn't tell him, did you?'

'Tell him what?' asked Nathan.

'You know – about me.'

'What about you?'

'You know,' she paused. 'About my… that I'm not...'

'Not normal – he'll find that out for himself.' Nathan laughed and headed to the picnic table.

'You better not have told him.' Nikki clenched her teeth but Nathan was now getting out the rolls and didn't seem to hear.

The creature tossed the emptied bag over her shoulder and turned to the frying pan that lay beside her. She held it right up to her nose, sniffing deeply and then licked the tantalising remnants of last night's cooking.

'Look, Nathan, you obviously don't wash up properly, she can smell sausages,' said Nikki, draping her wet fleecy on the tent guy ropes.

'Shut up. You do it next time,' said Nathan, handing a roll to the creature who stuffed it whole into her mouth.

Nikki woke three hours later in the boys' tent, lying across their lumpy feet. Chieftain was sleeping on her hair. She carefully slid him off and rubbed her stiff neck. She peeked out the tent flaps. Her tent remained closed up. She resisted checking on the creature, who'd gone to sleep on her bed, in case she woke and freaked. She got up, stretched and dumped the food pack on the picnic table. She sat there watching another camper trying to get his stove going. Soon the boys joined her.

'Don't look round, but some man's coming straight for us,' she hissed. Immediately, both boys looked over their shoulders. The man strode like an angry teacher, landing loud crunches on the gravel path, his glare fixed on Nikki. She sank lower over the table. Chieftain growled and slunk into the boys' tent.

'What the heck was all that noise last night? You woke up my whole family.'

I don't know him but I hate him, Nikki thought.

'Where are your parents?'

Nathan pointed to the caravan about twenty metres away in the bottom corner of the caravan park.

'What have you been taking? Alcopops? Beer?'

'No, of course not,' Nathan raised his voice.

But the man was not listening. 'Were you into our cold box as well? You made a hell of a mess.'

'But we didn't – ' Lyle began.

'If it happens again, I'll report you to the warden.'

'There was an animal – ' Nikki began.

'She got a fright, and – ' Lyle continued.

'I'm warning you, don't let it happen again,' the man interrupted.

Nathan stood up. 'Look, there's no need to accuse us, just because we're young.' But the man had already stalked off.

'We never went near your stuff,' Lyle shouted after him.

'What a…' Nathan began, but then sat down with a huff.

'He didn't even let us say anything, he just accused us.' Nikki's face felt hot with rage.

'The creature must have raided his food last night as well,' said Lyle.

They chewed their slightly stale rolls in silence for a moment, then movement in Nikki's tent told them that the creature had woken. She went to help her unzip the flaps.

Lyle said, 'We should decide what to do with the dog and the, eh… creature. We could ask around the campsite if anyone is missing a dog – '

'And a garden gnome,' Nathan joked and both boys laughed.

Nikki rolled her eyes. 'Will you two grow up?'

When they'd left, Nikki sat with the creature behind her tent and watched her examining a stone. Nikki noticed how her hair sprouted lower on the forehead than normal people's and wondered if she'd let her brush it – it'd be a great improvement. The creature had long lashes and a prominent eyebrow. True, some hair grew on her face – wispy sideburns and a little goatee, as the guys had so unkindly laughed about. The creature met Nikki's gaze with greenish brown eyes, very similar to Nikki's own colour. She noticed that there was less white in them than normal people's. The eyes narrowed and the creature tilted her head. She was doing it again – trying to see what Nikki wanted kept hidden. Nikki shuddered and looked away. Now she actually hoped that Nathan and Lyle would be back soon.

The creature raised a hairy, wrinkled hand towards Nikki's head. Nikki caught her by the wrist. What was she doing? The creature's gaze drifted up to Nikki's plastered forehead. Nikki released her, and said firmly, 'Just don't touch my hair.'

Pointing at Nikki's injury, the creature cooed sympathetically. Their eyes met again and this time Nikki could hold the gaze and the creature's face no longer appeared odd to her. She made no move to stop the creature from very gently lifting the corner of the plaster and peeling it back to expose the cut. She cooed again and cupped both hands over the wound without touching it. Nikki's forehead became warm and the warmth crept down her neck to her shoulders and through the rest of her body. She felt deliciously relaxed but she had to keep an eye on the creature. Her muscles couldn't seem to hold her up anymore and her eye lids were closing.

I've got to lie back. Try to stay awake... watch the creature...

'Nikki? Nikki?' she heard a distant voice.

Why are you bothering me? Let me sleep.

'Nikki, Nikki? Are you alright?'

She opened her eyes. Nathan was peering into her face. For a moment she thought she was in her bed at home. 'What?' She propped herself up on elbows.

Lyle squinted his chocolatey eyes. 'We thought you fainted, because of your head.' In an instant, Nikki took in his expression. His dark brows were dipped in concern and his mouth open as if waiting for her response before speaking. Did he really care? She glanced at Nathan who looked just as worried, but found herself preferring Lyle's attention.

'No, no, I'm fine. Where's the creature?' she said finally.

'Asleep in your tent,' said Nathan.

Nikki pulled back the flaps and peeked in. The creature was on her sleeping bag again, curled into the foetal position and sucking her thumb.

'No one reported a missing dog, but we didn't ask about a missing… well, we didn't ask anything else,' Lyle told her, grinning mischievously.

Nikki yawned. 'Then we should walk the dog into the village to see if anyone's put up any "missing" notices for him, or even for her.'

'What do we do if there's a dog "missing" notice, do we say, *we found a black Lab, but are you also missing a freak?* No offence to the creature, but we don't know what exactly it is,' said Lyle.

Nikki touched her hairline and shuddered. *Freak.* What would Lyle say about her, if he knew? Maybe he wasn't actually all that caring, after all. She said, 'Guys, of course we don't know, but she's good. I have this feeling that she's special. So unless anyone else has any better suggestions, I think we should get going.'

'We can't take the creature so I'll go and take the dog,' announced Lyle, standing up. 'The creature's asleep and you guys can handle her if she wakes up.'

'I'd quite like to go to the shop,' said Nikki, thinking that it might be easier to find out what Lyle was really like if Nathan wasn't around. They did seem to show off a little when they were together.

'But your head,' Nathan pointed at her plaster.

'It feels better now,' she said, vaguely puzzled that the throbbing had stopped. She peeled off the plaster, preferring to be seen in public with a cut rather than a plaster on her forehead.

'Oh,' said Lyle. 'It doesn't look as bad as I thought.'

Nikki frowned. 'I *did* fall asleep just then, and had a dream. The creature was in it. She put her hands on my forehead, and then it was better.' She shrugged. 'It seemed real.'

'Hmm,' said Lyle. 'Better get going then.'

'What'll I do if my mum or dad comes over while you're gone? What if they see the creature? They're just over there, remember,' said Nathan, pointing with his thumb.

'Well, maybe they can help. We haven't actually done anything wrong, you know,' said Nikki.

They set off down the single-track dirt lane that connected the campground to the main road. Her hand accidentally brushed against Lyle's. The touch was light and brief but she felt as if every nerve in her hand had sparked. It was a new and lovely sensation. She felt embarrassed, wondering if Lyle had felt it too and thereafter she kept her hands safely stuffed in her pockets or folded in front of her. She would've liked a lead for the dog, then she would have something to occupy her hand.

'It must be tough for Nathan, having his mum in a wheelchair,' said Lyle.

'Yeah. He has to help her a lot, so he doesn't get much spare time. His dad's doing all the looking after this trip, to give him a break.'

'I don't get much spare time either. I'm supposed to practise my cello for an hour a day and go to a Saturday Chinese class – all on top of homework. You know what Chinese parents are like.'

'How would I?'

'Most of the ones I know expect you to do really well at school and do a lot of extra stuff. What I'd really like to do is take up Tae Kwon Do with Nathan.'

'That gives him a break.'

'Has she always been in a wheelchair?'

'No, and the disease seems to come and go, so she doesn't always need it. Sometimes Nathan thinks it's his fault because the MS started after he was born.'

'How could it be his fault?'

'Of course it isn't. And his dad drinks too much because of it. Nathan hates that. But at least *his* dad's alive. Mine's dead.'

'Oh,' he said, and hesitated. 'Eh... sorry, I didn't know.'

'Yeah. But I kind of have two mums because of Nathan's mum. I call her Auntie Lynne.' She glanced at him and noticed how the sun gave his black hair a bluish gleam. Why was she telling him all this? He did look kind. Maybe it was his soft features. It might not be so bad having him around after all. Nevertheless, best not tell him anything else, she decided, and shoved her hands deeper into her pockets.

The traffic increased and Nikki walked behind Lyle, letting her arms swing free. After two miles they reached a pavement and the string of houses known as the village of Balicraig with its single shop, McKay's

Convenience Store. A few cards were stuck haphazardly in the window. The only "missing" notice was for a black cat.

Lyle waited outside with the dog. A bell jingled as Nikki entered the dingy little shop, which smelled of newspaper ink and chocolate. It seemed to sell everything on a small scale.

'Morning, pet,' the plump, elderly shopkeeper greeted her from behind the counter.

'Hi,' said Nikki, heading for the cold drinks.

The shop's radio was on: *'A seventy five year old woman has been shot dead in her Berkshire home.'* The shopkeeper turned up the sound. *'The body was found earlier today by the woman's home help, who has confirmed that nothing seems to be missing from the house. Villagers are shocked by this brutal and apparently motiveless murder of a well respected member of the community.'*

The shopkeeper tut-tutted. 'Who'd want to kill an old lady? Terrible.'

Nikki put the cokes, crisps and a local map on the counter. 'Do you know if anyone's lost a black Labrador?'

'No, Pet. But let's have a look in the local paper,' and she popped one on the counter and opened it to find the appropriate section. After a moment she said, 'There's nothing in here. Is that the Lab outside?'

'Yeah.'

'Try to catch the bin men. They've just been past. They have a scanner, so if the dog's been micro-chipped, they can get you the address.'

'They have a scanner?'

'Yes, it's so that they can scan any dead cats they find along their routes.'

'Nice,' said Nikki dolefully.

'Better run if you're going to catch them.'

Lyle approached a man swinging a wheelie bin into the lifting mechanism. 'Hi, I don't suppose you guys have one of those scanners for microchips do you?'

'Why y'askin'?'

'We found this dog,' Nikki replied.

'No collar, eh?' he said, and pulled off his dirty gloves to gently tug the dog's ear. 'Hey, Reggie, can ye git the scanner oot?' he called to the driver.

A moment later the scanner beeped over the dog's neck.

'That's a chip. It's showing up the ID number. Now I think we just need to ring the company to get the address. Not had to do this before.' He hopped into the cab to use the phone.

After a couples of minutes he told them, 'I'm no' supposed to give oot the details to a third party, but I suppose you're just planning on returning the dog.'

'Of course,' said Lyle.

'Well then, he lives at Eden House, Balicraig. I'll write it doon for you, and the phone number. The owner's name's been withheld.'

'Hey,' said the driver, 'you dinna want to go there. Some say a mad professor lives there and keeps a Frankenstein monster in his attic! But we don't believe it, do we lads!' He was laughing but sounded uncertain. 'Thank God he's a recluse.'

Nikki and Lyle exchanged looks. Nikki's mind raced – mad professor? So maybe the creature escaped from him, maybe she'd tried and tried and succeeded at last. Maybe they shouldn't return her. The creature looked nothing like Frankenstein's monster, but did he keep other strange creatures there?

The smaller man handed the scrap of paper to Nikki. She stared at the address. What had they got themselves into?

CHAPTER 4

Nikki found the creature squatting behind her tent, her rather monkey-like face and arms thankfully out of view from the campsite. Beyond her grew a few gnarled shrubs and then there was the stream. A thin twig dangled from the creature's lips, which flicked about when she glanced up at Nikki. Then she added the stick to others that lay arranged in a sun pattern in front of her. Nikki knelt on the shady grass and watched her alternate pebbles with the sticks. Behind her, she heard Lyle explaining about the scanner to Nathan.

She's definitely no monster, Nikki thought as the creature plucked a daisy and gave it to her.

'Look,' Nikki said, slitting the stem with her thumbnail. She threaded another daisy through the slot. 'It's a daisy chain.' The creature watched intently. Nikki threaded a third flower and laid it across the creature's outstretched and deeply lined hand. Nikki smiled, noticing the creature's eyes cross as she inspected it. 'You have a go.' But the creature tore the stem, shrieked and beat the ground with both fists. 'It's okay, it takes practice.' Nikki helped her to try again.

With a bottle of ketchup under his arm, Nathan brought over a plate of teetering hotdogs and a two litre bottle of Coke to the picnic table. The creature dropped the daisies, pushed off the ground with her fists and rushed over. Nikki sat opposite her and tried the phone number of Eden House for the third time, 'Still no answer.'

Nikki picked up her hotdog and was about to take a bite as she glanced across at the creature, whose hotdog had disappeared. Nikki stared at her bulging cheeks and tightly sealed lips from which sauce oozed like blood, and she had to turn away.

She dragged over the local map and spread it out. 'Look, here's Balicraig and our campground.' She traced her finger in a straight line. 'And there's Eden House. If we cut across those fields it'll be much faster than sticking to the roads.'

Nathan nodded and grunted with his mouth full. 'And Chieftain'll be happier away from cars.'

Nikki glanced at Lyle. 'Can we face another walk?'

'Sure, but not till after another hotdog.' He gave her a broad smile and she noticed some bread sticking to his very even white teeth.

As they set off, Nikki thought what an odd bunch they were – a lanky cat draped around Nathan's shoulders and a large dog walking at the heel of an unknown creature. Were they doing the right thing, bringing her back to a mad professor when she'd only just managed to escape? But what else could they do? At least they could take a look at the house and if it was really terrible and scary looking, they could just run away.

'So much for the short cut,' moaned Lyle, after half an hour of crossing fields.

'There should be a road at the end of this field,' said Nikki, glancing nervously at six long-haired highland cows that stared at them from a shady corner. The biggest one began to walk towards them and immediately the others followed.

'We'd better go a bit faster,' said Nathan, trotting. The cows began trotting too.

'They've got massive horns,' yelled Nikki, taking the creature's hand and running to the gate. She stumbled on the uneven ground moulded by hooves in the rain but now set hard. Behind her, thundering, like an inter-city train, told her that the cows were accelerating.

'Hurry, before we're trampled to death,' she yelled, narrowly missing a glistening cowpat. 'Faster, Lyle.'

Panting, they scrambled over the rickety wooden gate. Nikki watched Lyle slither over the gate just in time. The cows stopped abruptly a few feet away and blinked at them, breathing noisily through their huge nostrils. Nathan opened the gate just enough to let the dog through.

'That was close,' said Nikki, and glanced at the folded map. 'Eden House is just along to the right.'

They rounded a bend in the single-track road and ahead Nikki spotted a large white house surrounded by Scots pines and a stone wall. 'Is that your house?'

The creature nodded, her eyes and mouth drooping. Nikki's stomach gave a little churn – was she cruelly treated or was she just afraid of getting into trouble? Her mouth dried up as she wondered what the mad professor would say to them – or do to them! The house was completely isolated so no one would hear if they had to call for help. She glanced at the guys, glad not to be alone.

The name, "Eden House", was set into the low stone wall. With its bay windows on either side of the door, Eden House didn't look at all evil. The creature placed her hands on the wrought iron gate and gazed up at the dormer windows in the sloping roof. Her lips parted and Nikki thought she saw her eyes glistening. Then the creature put all her weight into pushing at the gate while it squeaked in resistance. Immediately, the dog forced his way past them, beating Nikki's legs with his tail.

'He's happy to be home, but I'm not too sure about her,' she said, and glanced at the driveway. 'No car, and all the curtains are open.' She stared at each of the windows, making sure that no one was peering out. Then she inhaled the cool pine scented air and followed the hand-like imprints made by the creature's bare feet in the thick mossy grass.

Nathan rang the bell. 'I wonder if we can get some water,' he gasped. 'My neck's hot and sweaty from having Chieftain there.'

'Ugh, that's disgusting. I don't want to touch him now,' Nikki complained, and stood back, glancing nervously into the room to the right of the door. Apart from the rectangles of light cast from the windows, the room was heavily shadowed. A sofa and a couple of armchairs had their backs to the window, in such a way that someone could sit there unseen from the window. While Nathan rang a second time, Nikki looked into the other room. It was just as dark and unwelcoming, with floor to ceiling bookcases displaying hundreds of colourless book spines. In fact, the only colour came from a large burgundy leather seat occupying the bay window. She held her breath wondering if the mad professor could be sitting deep within it, out of sight.

She felt the creature's hand slip into hers and since no one came to the door, she allowed herself to be led round the right side of the house and through a high wooden gate to the enclosed back garden.

'Wow,' she exclaimed. A lonely rope swing hung from a branch of one of several trees. An elaborate wooden climbing frame towered invitingly. But most special of all was the tree house complete with rope ladder, patio, door and windows. This was no mad professor's garden. Was all this hers or were there other kids?

The boys arrived and peered through the windows into the kitchen and utility room. Nathan said, 'No one's at home.'

Lyle knocked on the back door and the dog sat on the step. The creature grabbed the door handle, thrust a key into the lock and flung the door open.

'I never saw her get that,' exclaimed Nikki.

The dog waggled in first, sniffing and claws ticking on the cracked tiles. The creature vanished beyond the kitchen.

Nikki poked her head through the doorway. 'Hello, is anyone home?' No reply. 'We've just brought your dog back.'

She stepped in followed by Nathan and Lyle. 'Yuk,

it stinks in here,' she sneered. 'What a mess. Who did this?' Chieftain ran down Nathan's front and proceeded to sniff around the debris that littered the kitchen floor. The dog gobbled up a sulphurous broken egg. The cat licked an empty packet of ham. She kicked it away. 'No, Chieftain, that's off!'

'Shush, listen,' said Lyle. A tap dripped. Chieftain meowed in the hallway.

'What do we do now?' asked Nathan.

'Well, we brought the animals back. Now let's just lock them in and go,' said Lyle, holding the door ready to close up.

Nikki rolled her eyes. 'We can't just leave them unless there's someone to look after them and it smells as if this mess has been here for days.' She closed an open cupboard with her foot. 'Maybe there's no one here and they had to raid for food.'

'Okay, we could check the place out. The mad professor might be lying dead somewhere,' said Nathan.

'Shut up,' said Nikki, stepping over the strewn mouldy bread and half eaten carrots on her way to the hall.

'Nikki, you check the downstairs, while we go up,' he said.

Great, she thought, standing alone in the hall. The boys' feet clumped on the stairs. Behind her the kitchen tap continued to drip and the dog's tongue licked at long empty packets. The house was cold and she shivered. She felt as if they'd broken in. What if someone suddenly appeared?

She paused at the living room door. What if there

were a dead body in there? Butterflies formed in her stomach. She'd seen a dead body before – her dad's.

Two armchairs faced the empty fireplace. Heart thudding, she tiptoed to peek into them. Chieftain was sitting on one. She stroked him, amused at herself. If there *were* a dead body in the house, would Chieftain be acting so normal?

From inside, the room didn't look so dark and unfriendly, just old fashioned with its cabinet displaying gaudy old china and the uncomfortable looking, faded floral sofas with their poorly arranged, mismatched cushions. This was no family living room. No sign of toys. So unlike the garden.

Any clues on the mantelpiece? She picked up the ornately carved clock. It was as if time had stopped in this room the moment the clock fell silent. Could have been years ago, judging by what was in the room.

Suddenly, a hand gripped her arm. She screamed.

'Oh, it's you.' She looked into the creature's bright eyes. 'I didn't hear you come in.' The dog, also silent, followed the creature, brushed past Nikki and slumped by the cold hearth.

Nathan called to her from somewhere, 'Definitely no one in the house. We're going to check outside.'

'Okay,' she shouted back.

The creature reached a long arm up to the mantelpiece, pulled down a photograph and handed it to Nikki. She studied the picture of a man in a cap holding a fishing rod in one hand and a large fish hung below the other. A black Lab was with him.

The creature pointed to the man in photo and with

her finger wrote 999 in the thin layer of ash on the hearth tiles.

Nikki stared, her mouth open. 'Is he in hospital?' The creature nodded. 'Does he look after you?' The creature nodded again. 'Does anyone else live here?' The creature pointed to the dog. 'Do any other people live here?' The creature shook her head.

'What's the dog's name?' Nikki asked, wondering if the creature could reply. But she simply took the photo from Nikki and turned it over. Untidy cursive handwriting stated: "Henry and Einstein with 15 lb salmon, June 2005". She pointed to the name "Einstein".

'So you can understand everything.' Smiling, Nikki squatted down to the creature's height. 'What's *your* name?'

The creature grinned and jumped up. She yanked open a drawer under the coffee table and fished out a pen and paper. Leaning on the table, she stuck her tongue out in concentration and slowly printed some wobbly letters: *CHEEKA*.

'Let me see,' said Nikki. 'Cheeka. I like it.' With a name, Cheeka became a person. 'Are you cheeky, Cheeka?' Cheeka grinned and made a kind of laughing noise.

Nikki asked her usual second question for small children: 'How old are you?' and Cheeka held up four fingers.

'I need a last name,' she muttered, heading to the front door. She picked up the slithering heap of mail. "Professor Henry Ivanson" was on all the envelopes.

'Cheeka, if he's in hospital, who's meant to be looking after you?'

Cheeka stuck out her bottom lip.

Judging from the oldest postmark, the mail hadn't been looked at for five days, so Cheeka and Einstein must have been alone for that long. Maybe no one else knows there's a... well...a kind of a child here, Nikki thought, all alone – except for the dog. 'That certainly explains the state of the kitchen,' she muttered.

She heard the guys coming back from the garden. Nathan told her, 'No one's in the greenhouse or garage. Cool garden.'

Nikki blurted out: 'Cheeka's really clever. Cheeka – that's her name – she wrote it for me, and she told me only one man lives here and he's in hospital and his name's Professor Henry Einstein – no I mean Ivanson – Einstein's the dog, and the creature's name is Cheeka and she's four.'

Lyle laughed. 'Not so fast, Nikki.'

'You mean she *can* talk?' asked Nathan.

'No, she just pointed to the names. But it's really great that she can actually communicate.'

'There's a kid's bedroom upstairs at the back. Maybe it's hers,' said Nathan.

Cheeka grabbed Nikki's hand and dragged her upstairs and into the first room on the right. Nikki rubbed her shoulder – Cheeka was surprisingly strong.

Clothes, books and soft toys lay strewn all over the floor. Under the window at the back stood a toddler bed with a bunched up quilt and pillow.

'Hey Cheeka, don't you ever put anything away?'

Cheeka jumped on a brightly coloured beanbag, compressing it even more than it was already. Then she shot over to her little table that occupied pride of place at the centre of her room and quickly drew something on a paper pad. Several other specimens of her work were stuck to the walls. Many featured stick people with coloured outlines around them, like halos, only around the whole body. Nikki fished out her mobile phone and took some pictures of her.

'Hey, Nikki,' Nathan yelled up the stairs. 'We'd better head back. My dad's doing a barbecue for us.'

Cheeka slid down the banister ahead of Nikki and almost crashed into Nathan who stood at the bottom.

'What do we do about the beasts?' asked Lyle.

Nikki groaned. 'They're not beasts and Cheeka isn't an animal, Lyle. And we bring them, of course.' He doesn't seem to care about animals much, she thought.

'What, to the barbecue?' asked Nathan, frowning.

'No, we leave them in the tents,' replied Nikki.

'Do we tell my mum and dad about... all this?' asked Nathan.

'There must be someone to call, a neighbour or a friend.' Lyle glanced at Nikki with a mischievous glint in his eye. 'RSPCA?'

Nikki rolled her eyes and shook her head. Perhaps he was just trying to wind her up.

'There aren't any neighbours,' said Nathan.

'And he's a recluse, remember? Cheeka, d'you have any friends?' asked Nikki, and Cheeka shook her head. 'How about we phone the hospital? Then at least we might find out what to do from the professor. He might even be...' and she mouthed the word "dead".

Lyle said, 'I vote Nikki phones. Our voices could squeak and give away our age.'

Before Nikki could answer, Nathan asked, 'If he is in fact – *d – e – a – d* – then I suppose we should try the police or social services.'

Not finding a phone in the hall, Nikki pushed open the study door and immediately noticed a ladder hanging on the bookcase opposite. She slid it a little way along its runner. It seemed safe enough, but not being great with heights, she only climbed part way up. Movement on the mantelpiece caught her eye. It was Chieftain perched on an old rectangular case covered in dark leather.

'What's in there, Chieffers?' She climbed down, lifted him off and opened it. There, lying in grubby cotton wool, were three old skulls. She stared at the zigzag joins of the craniums and then lifted them out and arranged them on the desk. They grinned liplessly and stared blindly back at her from huge empty eye sockets. Smiling, she stood back and took their photograph. Then, setting her phone on the mantelpiece, she pulled off her hoody, grabbed a skull and dressed it in the hood. She tiptoed out and peeked at the boys from behind the living room door. They were lying back in the armchairs.

'Ohhhhh, wahhhh,' she wailed from behind the door, waving the hooded skull into the room.

Nathan and Lyle went silent for a second then laughed.

'Where did you get that?' asked Lyle, coming over for a look.

'Come and see the rest,' she said, handing him the skull.

Lyle placed the skull back with the others on the desk. 'They're all different,' he said.

'Look, it's a sequence,' said Nathan. 'This one, with the biggest brain box, is human.'

'Yeah, it has a chin. Only humans have a proper chin,' added Lyle.

'And this one, with the fangs and big brow, must be an ape or chimp,' said Nathan.

Nikki picked up the middle one. 'This one looks about half way between the other two.'

'Exactly,' said Nathan.

'It must be an early human. The cranium is smaller than ours and it still has the big brow,' said Lyle.

'Uhh?' said Cheeka, from the study doorway.

Nikki looked at her. Then she looked at the skull in her hand. Her mouth dropped open. She looked at Cheeka again and then at Nathan and Lyle. 'Are you thinking what I'm thinking?'

'You don't think – no – she can't be…' said Nathan.

'A human ancestor?' gasped Nikki.

'Don't be so stupid, if she's alive now, how can she be an ancestor?' he said. Nikki turned away, her face becoming hotter. Why did she have to say such naff things?

'Well, where did it come from? Did he find it on some expedition or did he make it in his lab?' Lyle sounded bewildered.

Nathan shook his head. 'This is all too weird.'

'What if he made her?' asked Nikki, staring into the skull's empty sockets.

'He's probably some kind of evil scientist,' said Lyle, his dark eyes flashing.

'Yeah. Anyway, it isn't normal for an old man to

keep a semi-human creature as a pet,' said Nathan.

'He didn't even get anyone to look after her,' added Nikki.

'He could be torturing her or doing experiments on her,' said Nathan. 'This place is starting to give me the creeps. Let's get going.'

Einstein appeared in the doorway, whining.

'Maybe he's hungry. Let's find some dog food while Nikki phones,' said Nathan.

Nikki carefully replaced the skulls in their cotton padded coffin. She found two hospitals listed in the slim phone book and underlined the number for the nearest one – in Portree. She made her enquires using her most grown up voice. In the margin of the phone book she wrote: *Ward 3* and *visiting 11 am – 12 pm, 4 – 5* and *7 – 8*.

She found the boys in the kitchen, watching Einstein eat. She told them, 'He's in the hospital in Portree. The receptionist couldn't tell me what's wrong with him. I said I was a neighbour.'

'Only, there are no neighbours.' Nathan grinned.

Ignoring him, she continued, 'She said that patients have phones by their beds, but I didn't want to speak to him. We could visit tomorrow just to take a peek and see what he's like.'

Nathan grunted and shrugged. Nikki took that to be a "yes".

'I'll grab some of Cheeka's things, then we can go,' she said.

In Cheeka's room she found a little backpack and wondered what to bring. Cheeka snatched it away and stuffed in a few random items. In the bathroom Nikki found a child's toothbrush - but why, when Cheeka didn't exactly have child-sized teeth? Then Cheeka sat on the toilet so Nikki left. 'See you by the back door.'

The guys weren't in the kitchen, but something moved behind the frosted glass of the back door. Nikki halted - someone was coming - someone much bigger than the guys. Her heart thudded. Was the professor back? Was someone checking the house? Was it a burglar? Had they locked the door?

She slid along the wall, dropped below the frosted window and turned the latch as quickly and quietly as she could. She crouched below the window and hoped that the door wouldn't be kicked down.

The daylight above her head dimmed. Someone was right there! Her heart did a few double beats. She stole a glance upwards. A huge dark form rippled behind the frosted glass. Inches from her head, the door handle vigorously rattled.

CHAPTER 5

The figure retreated, feet crunching on gravel. Nikki slowly exhaled. She was about to get up when a man's shadow appeared on the wall opposite the sink. She dared not move. The shadow rocked from side to side as if he was trying to see into the corners of the kitchen. The window frame was knocked and banged, shaking the patch of light on the wall. Nikki pressed herself against the door. Since the owner wasn't home, there would be nothing to stop him from breaking in. She willed the guys and Cheeka not to come, if they did, he'd see them, and what then?

She saw the shadow turn and at the same time she glimpsed Cheeka heading towards the kitchen. She whisked a finger to her lips and held up a hand asking her to stay back. At last the crunching sound told her that the man was leaving. She shot from the kitchen, grabbing Cheeka's hand, and called as loudly as she dared, 'Hey guys, where are you?'

'Up here,' one answered.

She took the stairs two at a time, dragging Cheeka.

'Someone's just been banging on the kitchen windows. He tried the back door – I got it locked just in time. He's gone around the front.' She followed the boys into a front bedroom and said, 'If it was just someone checking on the house, wouldn't they have a key?'

They peered from behind the long checked curtain, to see a man with dark clothes and a shaved head stride down the drive towards a black car parked beside the garden wall. His size and mirrored sunglasses gave him a monstrous and almost robotic look.

'A Maserati GranTurismo. Nice,' remarked Nathan.

'Probably just a neighbour,' said Lyle.

'What neighbours?' groaned Nathan.

'He must be a burglar – he was so rough with the window and door,' said Nikki. 'And the house is so isolated.'

'But most of the houses on Skye are isolated, so why choose this one? And why would a burglar bang on the window and then leave when clearly no one's home?' remarked Nathan. 'The car window's opening.'

Smoked glass descended exposing a dark figure first aiming binoculars at the upper windows, and then speaking into a mobile phone. Immediately, they retreated behind the curtain. Seconds later, the engine started and they watched the car take off, wheels spinning, sending out a cloud of dust from the grassy verge.

'Does seem a bit weird,' said Nathan.

'Maybe he just wants to buy the house, or something,' said Lyle, but Nikki detected the doubt in his voice.

That night, Nikki shared her mattress with Cheeka and used the opened out sleeping bag as a quilt. Chieftain slept on her feet. Lyle had said this camping spot had the best *feng shui* because the flowing water meant that money would flow their way. Good *feng shui* or bad, that stream was keeping her awake, again. She lay listening to the dog's snoring outside her tent. It sounded disconcertingly human. But as for Cheeka, she's disconcertingly non-human, she thought. Can I fall asleep with her beside me? What if she wakes up and stares at me while I'm sleeping? What if she does something to me while I'm asleep? Don't think about the skulls. Don't think about the strange man or mad professors. Don't think about weird experiments and no wondering about what Cheeka might be.

At last sleep enveloped her, like a bath of melted chocolate.

Nikki stood by the professor's bedside. She could see a bald head – almost as white as the pillow it rested on. 'Cheeka's here to see you,' she said. The professor's head turned to face her. It was the skull!

She woke with a frightened start before the filtered green daylight through the tent walls reassured her. Her pyjama top was damp with the sweat of a scary night's dream. She glanced around – the unzipped door flapped open and Cheeka and Chieftain were gone.

Outside, she found Cheeka sitting cross-legged on the damp grass with Chieftain eating from a pile of dried cat food in front of her. Cheeka was crunching loudly and her lips were covered with crumbs. Nikki shook her head and sighed.

As soon as the boys emerged from their tent, Nikki handed them each a breakfast bar and announced, 'We have to go to the hospital today. Me and Nathan can pretend to be the grandchildren. Lyle could be a friend, like he is already.'

'But I'd rather stay behind,' Lyle said quickly.

'In that case, you can look after Cheeka,' said Nikki.

Before Lyle could reply, they heard an angry wail. Turning, they saw Cheeka standing with clenched fists and her daypack on. Her teeth were bared and lips pulled back in the same angry grimace they'd seen when they first met.

'It's okay, Cheeka, maybe you can go another day. They might not let small children into the hospital,' Nikki explained.

Cheeka wailed again and stamped over to the main path, seeming not to notice the stones under her bare feet.

'What can we do?' asked Nikki. 'He's her guardian – maybe we shouldn't stop her.'

'Okay, let's all go. I don't want to deal with *that* sort of thing anyway,' said Lyle.

Nikki looked at Cheeka's large, hairy, hand-like feet and decided that she couldn't be seen in public like that. 'Come on, Cheeka, I'll get you my spare trainers.'

'I'll leave Chieftain in the caravan with mum this time. I'll drop by the warden to find out when the bus comes,' said Nathan.

In her tent, Nikki stretched a pair of socks over Cheeka's wide feet and pulled them high enough to hide her hairy ankles. The trainers looked ridiculously big, but they'd have to do. She put one of her own hoodies on Cheeka because it was bigger and would hide more of her face. Cheeka's arms were so long that she didn't have to roll up the sleeves. Then she rummaged to the bottom of her backpack.

'Don't be scared. Do you know what this is?' she asked, switching on her shaver.

'Uhh.'

'See how it works.' Nikki demonstrated on her own leg, then she slowly approached Cheeka's chin, but Cheeka screamed and fled the tent.

'What's going on?' Nathan was obviously back. 'We should leave now, there's a bus in twenty minutes. They only come by every hour and we have walk to the main road.'

Cheeka squealed and jumped up and down when the bus rumbled round the corner. Nathan waved for it to stop. While he paid, Nikki made sure that Cheeka's hood was securely done up and smiled at the unusual little face. Cheeka pulled away, clambered in and ran down the aisle, too quickly, Nikki hoped, for the six other passengers to notice what she looked like. Laughing, Cheeka bounced up and down on the back seat and Nikki wondered if she would be able to keep her under control. She supposed this was her first ever bus ride.

'This could turn out to be a big mistake,' moaned Nathan. He and Lyle sat each side of the second back row to act as guards lest she try to run to the front. The journey seemed to take forever on the twisting roads. Cheeka leapt from one side of the bus to the other, rarely sitting still for more than a minute, seemingly interested in everything from people on bicycles to grazing sheep. With Cheeka's activity and the swaying bus, Nikki was feeling more and more sick.

'If we have to come again, we take a taxi,' she groaned.

At last the bus swung into its parking slot in Portree's town square but Nikki's stomach had already started to heave. She fought to suppress it. Cheeka swung from pole to pole like an agile monkey, propelling herself towards the front.

I'm going to explode! Incapable of excusing herself, Nikki shoved past the other passengers and fled to a nearby barrel of planted flowers where she vomited, unable to care about the pansies or who saw her.

'This isn't how I wanted to spend our camping holiday,' Nathan grumped.

Guys can be so insensitive, she thought, wiping sick from the corner of her mouth. Then, spotting a sign for the hospital, she grabbed Cheeka's hand and crossed over to walk along the main shopping street, which actually consisted of only about ten shops on each side. She glanced at a window display of Celtic jewellery and decided she'd have to come back another day for a proper look around. Ahead of them, sailboats dotted the glistening sea; perhaps some were headed for the island whose hazy mountains looked purple in the distance.

'It's really small,' said Lyle, as they turned into the tiny jammed-packed hospital car park.

'What did you expect?' said Nikki, looking at the two-story building. She pushed open the door. At the reception desk she asked, 'Where's Ward Three please?' She sounded brighter than she felt.

'Up the stairs, down the corridor and it's the last door on the right,' the woman replied.

'We should bring him something,' Nikki mumbled, entering the tiny gift shop next to the single lift. She caught sight of her own reflection in the security mirror. Her hair was still intact but the ordeal had left her far too pale. She wished she looked older, but there was a way... She chose some mascara and lipstick, and grabbed a bunch of flowers for the professor and four bars of chocolate. She sniffed the fresh blooms and felt better.

'I'm just taking Cheeka to the *ladies*.' Here she inspected her hairline in the mirror and arranged her fringe to cover it. Then she got out the makeup. Chewing chocolate and sitting up by the sink, Cheeka watched her every move.

Through the Perspex doors leading to Ward Three, a nurse with red hair scraped into a bun, spotted them and blocked their entry. 'Sorry, visiting time's just ended.'

Nathan stepped forward and said, a little too aggressively for Nikki's liking, 'Look, we've come on an hour long bus ride that made my cousin puke, and we are not leaving until we've seen our grandfather.'

The nurse inhaled sharply and Nikki blushed but tried to look ill.

'What's his name?' The nurse relented.

'Professor Ivanson,' Nikki replied quietly.

The nurse looked surprised. 'Oh, we understood from his GP that he had no family – must be a mistake.

Glad you're here. As you may know, your grandfather's had a stroke,' she paused, as if expecting a reaction. Receiving none, she continued, 'He's got weakness down his left side and he's in and out of consciousness – mostly out. He can talk, although a lot of it doesn't make sense. Where are your parents?'

'Oh, um – they'll come later,' said Nikki, moving to shield Cheeka from her the nurse's stare. 'They're at work. Schools are out so we came see him.'

'Hmm. Okay, I'll take you to him.'

Nikki blinked with relief. She doubted she'd recognise him from the outdated photo. What would he be like? He sounded mad. Would he be able to tell them who could look after Cheeka and Einstein?

'I hope he can answer some questions about the creature. We have the right to ask, since we're looking after it,' Lyle whispered, and Nikki wished he wouldn't keep on calling Cheeka "the creature" and "it".

The nurse paused at the foot of the old man's bed and spoke softly, 'He's often confused. Sometimes it's as if he's living in a nightmare – thinking that someone's out to get him. Other times he keeps saying he has to go home to take care of something. Has he a pet?'

'A dog,' Nikki and Nathan almost shouted together.

'Will he ever get better?' Nikki glanced at Cheeka, who was tugging to get free.

'Time will tell. Luckily he got here soon after he collapsed. It's amazing he managed to call the ambulance himself. Apparently he just dialled and grunted. The call had to be traced.'

'Uhh,' said Cheeka.

'Um – will she behave in here?' asked the nurse, frowning suspiciously.

Nathan glared at her. 'She'll be fine.'

The nurse left, calling over her shoulder, 'Don't be too long with him.'

Nikki released Cheeka who catapulted towards the professor's bed. Nikki slowly approached the blanketed mound. On the pillow the shining bald head lay surrounded by a ring of untidy grey hair, rather like her dream. The nose was slightly hooked and the eyes closed in sleep. The virtually white, neatly cropped beard contrasted with the black eyebrows that were long and curled as if his habit was to twist them whilst in thought.

'He looks about the same age as Grandpa Adams,' observed Nikki. 'Except he's thinner.' She felt the nurse's eyes burning into the back of her head and whisked the privacy curtains right around the bed. Cheeka whimpered and held the professor's freckled hand. A tear trickled and absorbed into the hair under her chin. Nikki's eyes flooded in sympathy, Cheeka obviously loved him.

'It's okay, Cheeka, he'll be alright.' Nikki softly touched her shoulder but Cheeka shrugged free. 'Look, I brought flowers for him.'

Cheeka whirled round. She looked angry. She snatched the flowers and ripped them to shreds. Torn petals and leaves showered her feet.

'What on earth?' Nathan's mouth hung open.

'She's weird, definitely very weird,' said Lyle, shaking his head. 'Aren't you going to tell her off?'

Confused and hurt, Nikki scraped up the remains with her fingers and binned them.

Cheeka laid her hands on the professor's head. Her eyes closed and her brow wrinkled. It looked, to Nikki, as if she was trying to hear his thoughts through her hands. The hands shifted to new places until she had been over his whole head. She then pressed her hands to one area and began muttering. Nikki stared at the stranger sleeping in bed, and the kid, who wasn't exactly human, doing things to the man's head that she didn't understand.

'Let's get out of here,' said Nathan.

Suddenly Cheeka withdrew, unzipped her daypack and delved in.

Nikki hadn't seen her pack it. 'Oh no, what's in there?'

'Oh no,' whispered Lyle. 'She's brought some hocus-pocus stuff.'

'Stop her,' demanded Nathan, but already Cheeka was arranging pebbles on the pillow around his head.

'Cheeka, no!' Nikki gently pulled Cheeka's arm but she flicked her off, glaring. Was she going to go into one of her rages? By now Cheeka had laid alternating twigs and stones in a radial pattern around the professor's head. She pulled back the covers to reveal his mottled feet and proceeded to do the same there.

'Does she really know what she's doing?' Nikki asked, and then remembered her forehead. She touched the rapidly healing wound - what had Cheeka done there?

From her pack, Cheeka pulled out a plastic pot and

quickly opened it, revealing a stinking mash of mud and leaves.

'No, Cheeka,' Nikki said, and tried to take it from her, but Cheeka growled, showing a flash of her large white teeth. Nikki backed off. 'I can't stop her.'

'How are we going to get out of this?' asked Nathan.

'We might have to carry her out kicking and screaming,' Lyle groaned.

Muttering, Cheeka began to plaster the professor's head with mud, especially the area she'd chosen before.

'Nikki,' hissed Nathan, 'do something!'

'Oh no,' she groaned.

'This is a hospital,' exclaimed Lyle.

Nikki had visions of the police arriving.

'This is out of control,' groaned Nathan, 'we're way out of our depth here. We have to get out of this, now!'

'Yeah, well if you can see a way out, please show me, because I have no idea what to do!' Nikki glowered, but before their argument could escalate, briskly approaching footsteps sounded.

Nathan slipped his head between the curtains. 'Oh no, Nurse is coming.'

On the spur of the moment, Nikki faked loud crying.

Nathan popped his head again. 'My cousin's a bit upset, please can we have a few more minutes?'

'Five.'

'Nathan, get some paper towels and wet some so we can clean him up,' hissed Nikki.

'No, let's just leave him and get out of here.'

'Who knows, it might actually cure him,' said Lyle.

'Then we can never come back,' said Nikki.

'I don't ever want to come back,' Nathan said, but then relented. 'Okay, okay, I'll do it.'

Nathan slipped out just as the old professor stirred. Cheeka took a step back.

By the time Nathan came back with the towels, the professor was struggling to open his eyes. Drying mud cracked as his cheek muscles contracted. Was it Cheeka's treatment or even just her presence that brought him round? His dark eyes squinted and his face broke into a lopsided smile. Lumps of mud and leaves dropped off onto the pristine white pillowcase. He chuckled and reached for Cheeka with his right arm. The left arm lay lifeless beside him. His eyes moistened.

'Cheeka, my Cheeka, are you safe?' he squeaked. 'Are you alright?'

Cheeka lifted her hands and moved her fingers at speed.

Nikki whispered, 'She's using sign language - of course the professor would've taught her that. She's intelligent and can understand everything - just can't talk.'

'Is Liz taking care of you? How did you get here?' The professor sounded very concerned.

Cheeka fingers were almost a blur with movement.

'Why didn't you phone Liz? I told you to phone Liz and play her the message if something happened to me.'

'We're looking after her at the moment, Professor Ivanson.'

The professor squinted at Nikki. 'Liz?'

'No. My name is Nikki Tollik and this is my cousin Nathan Adams and our friend Lyle Cheung. We found Cheeka and Einstein, yesterday, at our campsite. She led us to your house and let us in. That's how we found out you were here.'

'How long have I been here?'

'A few days, I think,' she said.

'I must get out of here, Cheeka needs me.' He tried to move, but nothing happened. Nikki saw the distress in his eyes.

'Who's Liz? Should we call her to look after Cheeka?'

'My sister. It's a bit late now – it would take her a couple of days to get here. I'll be out by then.'

'How about someone on Skye?' asked Nikki.

The professor clutched her arm with his good hand. 'There's no one. No one I can trust,' he wheezed. 'You look so young, how old are you?'

Nikki hesitated, then stood as tall as she could. 'Sixteen,' she lied, glad of the makeup. She hated lying – it always made things worse. But if she'd said thirteen the professor might not have trusted her to look after Cheeka, not that the guys would've cared. He might not answer their questions either.

'You're already looking after her? I'm so grateful. Will you take care of her a little longer? Keep her safe. Bit of a temper... but she won't bite... I can't... I can't...' The old man lost his grip on Nikki, his head tilted and his eyes closed. She gently returned the dangling arm to the bed.

'Oh no, I think he's stopped breathing!' she whispered. 'The nurse'll think we killed him with the mud!' Her heart thumped and her eyes searched the mound for any sign of chest movement.

After a few seconds, the professor took a gulp of air. Nikki's heart made a double beat. After a few seconds, he started breathing properly again.

'Thank God for that,' she said.

'He's okay now. Let's go,' said her cousin, sounding agitated.

'I want to clean him first,' she said, taking the damp paper towels from him. She attempted some gentle wipes at the mud plaster on his face and head. The professor opened his eyes and gripped her wrist again. She squealed.

'Leave the mud,' he wheezed. 'The poultice needs time to work. I don't know how it works but it does.'

'Nurse is coming,' said Lyle.

'Cover my head,' said the professor. Nikki quickly draped a hospital towel to cover most of his head and mud smeared cheeks.

'Time up.' The nurse didn't even look at them or stay to see them off.

The professor's eyes rolled and he looked up at Nikki. 'Keep her hidden, keep her safe,' he rasped. 'Danger. She's in danger…'

'What do you mean, *danger*?' Nikki asked quickly. But he'd drifted into unconsciousness before revealing more.

CHAPTER 6

Nikki quickly wrote the professor's bedside phone number on the back of her hand, then tightened up Cheeka's hood and whisked her up to carry her. They dashed out, leaving the curtains swinging.

'We've got away,' said Nathan, as the entered the corridor.

'Wait!' cried the nurse, bustling after them.

'Oh no, she's found the mud,' Lyle groaned.

Breathless, the nurse caught them up. 'You didn't give me your phone number.'

Nikki stared blankly, holding Cheeka to face away from the nurse.

'I'll need to be in touch with your parents about your grandfather.'

'Oh, okay,' said Nikki, and gave her the mobile number.

'Thank you. And your home number? Obviously, it's your parents I need to speak to.'

'Uh…' Nikki hesitated.

'We're just here on holiday,' said Nathan. 'So they don't have a phone. They just borrow our mobile.'

'I thought you said they were at work?'

'Yeah – a business conference – if it's any of your business,' said Nathan.

The nurse scowled and looked Nathan up and down.

'Excuse us,' Lyle said to the nurse, 'but we have to run for the bus.'

Nikki felt a warm hand on her elbow; Lyle was turning her around but quickly released her.

'What an old bag she is,' Nathan snorted, as they hurried off.

'I can still feel her staring,' said Nikki, also still feeling the touch that Lyle had left on her arm.

'Let's run before she finds the mud,' said Lyle.

'Wish I could see her face when she does,' said Nathan.

On the bus they had a few more snickers about nurses, mud and lies before falling silent. Sunrays streamed through the window and Nikki's gaze drifted over a green valley dotted with grazing sheep and the occasional white farmhouse. The air was becoming hotter and Cheeka leaned up against her. Coloured blooms in a small roadside cemetery caught her eye and she remembered Cheeka wrecking the professor's flowers - were they a symbol of death for her? And what did the professor mean about Cheeka being in danger? Was he just raving like the nurse said? She glanced at the guys, but seeing their lolling heads and open mouths, she let them sleep. They looked quite cute, sleeping like little boys.

Free at last from the stifling atmosphere of the bus, they headed back to camp on the dusty single-track road. Cheeka took Nikki's hand. A cool breeze lifted Nikki's fringe and, glancing at Lyle, she tried to smooth it down. Since the guys were looking more alert, she challenged them with the question of Cheeka's danger.

'Could it have anything to do with the man who

came to the house?' she asked.

'How would we know?' replied Nathan. 'We don't even know that the professor's good.'

'Yeah, she could be in danger from him,' Lyle pointed out.

Nikki said, 'But he must be good – he really cares about Cheeka. Think of all the stuff she has.'

'Did you know that people kept captive in a basement or wherever, actually become attached to the person keeping them prisoner?' said Lyle.

'That's ridiculous,' said Nathan.

'Yeah, it's weird, but true. I heard it on the news. Probably it's just because they have no one else.'

'So, just because Cheeka loves the professor, it doesn't mean he's not cruel to her?' asked Nikki.

'Exactly. But then – she isn't really human, is she?' said Lyle.

Nikki winced and glanced at Cheeka. True, she wasn't like them, but she wasn't like an animal.

'Yeah, but even dogs can love cruel masters,' said Nathan.

They walked in silence for a moment. Cheeka pulled off her hood revealing hair that was becoming more and more tangled. She looked up into Nikki's eyes and grinned. That's definitely a human thing to do, Nikki thought, and she can understand everything we say. She loves the professor and she even cried. But where did she come from and how could she be in danger?

Lyle broke the silence. 'We should phone the professor's sister, then she can take over as soon as she gets here.'

'There'll be an address book at his house,' said Nikki. 'You know, if Cheeka's in danger, maybe that's why he can only trust his sister to look after her – and us, of course.'

'We should check around his house for any signs of him being cruel,' said Nathan.

'What if he is?' asked Nikki.

'We could call social services,' Nathan replied.

'Or the RSPCA,' said Lyle.

'Either, as long as *we* don't have to look after her. I'm taking a break from that sort of thing,' said Nathan.

'Well, I want to help her. You can't just not bother to care about things just because you're on holiday, you know,' said Nikki.

'Oh, aren't you great. And, by the way, I think I know a hell of a lot more about caring than you – '

Lyle interrupted, 'Wouldn't it be really cool to find out exactly what kind of creature she is? If she really is like some kind of human ancestor that he found in a jungle, then it's a really important discovery.'

'On the other hand, she might just be his mutant grandchild, dumped on him by her parents,' grumped Nathan.

An hour later, they were standing in the professor's gloomy study.

'What kind of professor do you think he is?' asked Nikki, running her hand along a dusty bookshelf, scanning the incomprehensible titles.

'Something to do with science or anthropology,' said Nathan, lifting a new-looking science issue from the desk.

'Remind me what anthropology is?' asked Nikki, picking up his floral address book.

'The study of early humans,' Lyle said from behind the computer on the desk. 'You know, their bones and stuff they left behind. He has those skulls remember? Maybe that's why he's interested in the creature – if she really is some kind of missing link – *very* interesting.' The computer hummed into life. 'I wonder if we can access anything on this.'

'Yeah, she is interesting.' Nikki hoped that Lyle was becoming fonder of Cheeka. 'She can draw and she speaks sign language – '

'No, I mean *interesting* because her brain might be like our ancestors' brains – like she can understand, but not talk.' Lyle spoke quickly while he clicked on the keyboard. 'Maybe there's something about the creature on here.'

Nikki watched his expressions as he spoke, with his dark eyes darting over the computer screen. He's much more mature than Nathan, she thought, really clever – but without being a nerd. If he was good at maths too, maybe she could ask him to help her next term.

Lyle continued, 'He's downloaded a file: *Humans and chimpanzees share 99% of their DNA – fact or fiction?* He could be a geneticist.'

'Know what I think?' she offered. 'Cheeka doesn't really seem like a four year old. She seems more mature and much less of a cry-baby. I've looked after small kids before, so I know.'

'Well, animals do grow up faster. Chieftain's two, so if he were human, he'd still be a baby,' Nathan added. 'But anyway, the prof could still be doing experiments with her – ones that don't hurt her. Observation of behaviour or intelligence tests – something like that.' He rummaged in a drawer. 'Oh, he's got some money here – a hundred quid.'

'Just leave it, Nathan,' warned Nikki.

'I'm not going to *steal* it. But I think we could borrow some to buy food for Cheeka.'

Nikki sighed. 'Well, I suppose we could borrow it to take a taxi the next time we visit him. If he is actually nice, he won't mind paying. After all, we're looking after Cheeka and Einstein.'

He stuffed the notes into his back pocket. 'He'd better get out soon – we're only here for a week. This could waste all our holiday.'

'Maybe Cheeka's potion will actually work,' said Nikki doubtfully.

Just then there was the sound of vigorous scratching.

'Chieftain's sharpening his claws on a carpet – I think he's upstairs,' she said, rushing out. Some red carpet fluff wafted on the top stair. All five doors on the upper landing stood ajar. She pushed open the first door on the left. Much of the space was filled by an enormous four-poster bed. Faded plum coloured curtains were tied back at the posts and the pillowcases didn't match the bedspread. With care, she stepped into the room. Dust particles swirled in a shaft of sunlight that streamed between the carelessly drawn curtains. A meow made her jump.

'Where are you, Chieffers?' She knelt down to look under the bed. He sat right at the back, blinking his reflective eyes at her. He sniffed the carpet and sneezed.

'Dusty, isn't it? Now come out.'

Ignoring her, he scratched at the carpet and a piece of it flapped up.

'What have you done?' She lay down and wriggled towards him. The square flap had been deliberately cut. She pulled it back exposing the floorboards. Maybe one was loose? She dug her fingers around the edges and lifted out a short plank. Chieftain sniffed inside the hole and sneezed again, spraying Nikki's hand. 'Yuk.'

Her hand hovered above the empty space – there could be spiders in there, this was an old house. Her heart quickened. She dragged herself forward just enough to peek in, but it was too dark to see. Slowly she dipped her fingers below the floor and touched paper. She lifted out a whole stack of them, wriggled back out and set them in front of her. Chieftain sat on them and looked as if he was grinning at her. She wiped her dusty hands on her shorts and nudged him off.

'If you want me to check this out, you have to move.' And she blew the dust off the top sheet and read the heading. 'Hey guys, come and look at this – I think I've found something!'

The thumping from the stairs sounded like six people, not two.

'In here,' she called. 'I found all these papers in a hiding place under the bed.' She began to read aloud: 'Application for a Government Home Office Special Experiment Licence – Experiment Title: Genetically Engineered Chimpanzee-Human Hybrid Embryo Study.' Nathan snatched the document from her hands. 'Ahh, you gave me a paper cut.'

'Sorry,' he mumbled, with eyes on the paper. She

frowned, trying to understand the words that he reac

Application for a Government Home Office Speci Experiment Licence

Experiment Title: Genetically Engineered Chimpanzee-Human Hybrid Embryo Study
Applicant: Dr R. McBraidy
Aims: To develop new ways to repair damaged brain, skin or other tissues in patients.
Research Establishment: The Institute for the Advancement of Human Health
Methods: Under laboratory conditions, eggs would be removed from Chimpanzees, placed into plastic culture dishes and micro-injected with human DNA. The resulting chimpanzee-human (chuman) hybrid embryos would be fed a liquid rich in vitamins. After a few days of cell division, the chuman embryos would form a ball of cells. We plan to separate these cells from one another to form clones in order to expand their numbers. Embryonic stem cells from these cloned chuman embryos, which are destined to become brain or skin cells etc, will be plucked off and allowed to multiply as specialised tissues in separate dishes.
Benefits to people:
After 2 weeks of growing, the specialised types of cells, for example brain or skin, can be transplanted into damaged areas of the body in animal or human subjects. Any improvement in the subject's ability to move/walk or perform tasks will be monitored daily. This experimental approach avoids the ethical issues of using truly human embryos. It is unlikely that the cloned chuman embryos would survive long enough to ever develop into viable creatures.
For official use only:
Success or Failure of Application: *Failed/Rejected. Permission to do proposed experiments has been refused by the Government Home Office.* We find insufficient justification for this work. Other research establishments are already making substantial progress in nerve regeneration and skin repair without resorting to the, quite frankly, Frankensteinian use of human-animal hybrid embryos.
Warning: If this illegal work is undertaken it will lead to prosecution and prison sentencing.

Nathan looked up from the drooping paper, his mouth open.

Nikki didn't want to believe it. 'Is that… does that mean… ?'

'Of course, Cheeka's part human, part chimpanzee,' Lyle exclaimed.

'Is that where she came from? Was she made in that lab?' Nikki wondered. 'Did the professor make her there?'

'If she was made there, or anywhere, it was obviously illegal,' said Nathan, 'and that'll be why they're hiding away here.'

'Maybe he actually has a secret lab here, in a cellar or somewhere,' Lyle speculated.

'Hold on now guys, Professor Ivanson's name isn't even on that piece of paper,' Nikki pointed out.

'He might have changed it,' said Nathan. 'If he's so innocent, then why did he hide all these papers under the bed? Or maybe he just copied the idea off these other guys.'

Cheeka appeared in the doorway and tilted her head. 'Huh?'

'Hey, we shouldn't talk about it in front of her,' said Nikki.

'Take her out then,' Nathan suggested. 'Lyle and I can look through this lot to find out more.'

She took Cheeka to the kitchen where she found a packet of chocolate digestives that had survived Cheeka's earlier raids and brought it to share with the others.

Lyle took a biscuit and told her, 'It looks like someone

really was making hybrid embryos illegally.'

'Is there anything actually about her?' she asked, stroking Chieftain who was now curled up on the four-poster.

'We haven't found anything about making actual hybrid creatures from the embryos,' he answered.

Chieftain sat bolt upright and let out a throaty growl, staring out of the room.

'What's up, Chieffers?' Nikki asked.

Something banged on the front door.

'What the...?' said Nathan.

A man's voice shouted, 'Professor! Open the door! I know you're in there – I saw you at the window.'

CHAPTER 7

Nikki's heart pounded. 'This must be the danger the professor meant. I'm scared, what do we do?' Cheeka wrapped her arms right around Nikki's hips and squeezed hard.

'He must've seen one of us through the window,' said Lyle.

The man now banged on the back door. 'Open up, Professor! It's all over now. You know what I want. Just hand it over and I'll be gone.' The back door handle jiggled vigorously. Cheeka whimpered and yanked at Nikki's arm. Glass smashed.

'He's breaking in!' said Nikki, her mouth turning dry. 'We'd better hide.'

'Hey, Nathan,' Lyle whispered, grabbing his arm. 'There's two of us – we can handle him, can't we?'

'Don't be stupid, he could be armed,' hissed Nikki.

The back door creaked open. Glass tinkled onto the tiles and was crunched beneath shoes.

'Where's Chieffers?' she whispered, frantically scanning the room.

'Cats can take care of themselves,' Nathan replied. 'But why isn't the dog going mental?'

'Shush,' she said. Below, footsteps squeaked in the tiled hallway. 'I think he's heading for the study.'

Nathan said, 'Nikki, go and hide. We'll be fine. We just need to see what he's doing.'

What do you think you are doing? Nikki wanted to yell at him. She grabbed his sleeve and held it tight. 'The only thing you two need to do is *hide*.'

Lyle glanced at Nikki. 'It's okay; we'll just check it out. Keep her quiet.'

Cheeka whimpered and tugged Nikki's arm that grasped Nathan. Nikki let go and put her finger to Cheeka's lips.

The boys slipped out. Nikki clenched her teeth. What if the man finds them on the stairs? He might decide they have to die! She watched them creep across the hall and ease their way down the stairs, their backs to the wall. She looked around the professor's room. 'Where's the best place to hide? Somewhere I'll fit too.'

'Uhh.' She felt a strong grip take her wrist and Cheeka pulled her into the hall. Now there was no sign of the boys. She heard drawers opening in the study below. Cheeka yanked her arm towards her bedroom doorway and Nikki hoped the floorboards wouldn't creak. One did. She froze, not breathing. Cheeka pulled her hard into the room. Nikki breathed again, hoping that the man was making enough noise to cover any creaking sounds.

She obviously feels safest here, Nikki thought, but if he's after her – he'll guess this is her room. She tried to pull Cheeka back out but Cheeka was stronger.

Her heart thudded faster. 'We have to hide *now*, Cheeka.'

Cheeka released her and fiddled with something.

Nikki stared as the dresser slid unaided along the wall to reveal a little doorway into darkness. Her mind flashed briefly to Earth House, but then Cheeka shot in and switched on a light. Nikki crouched through after her. Cheeka pulled a lever and a well-oiled mechanism silently slid the door, and the ingeniously attached dresser, to seal them in.

'What a fantastic hiding place.'

'Uhh.'

Nikki acutely listened for activity beyond their walls, but it was their own panting breath that filled her ears. Would she even hear anyone coming into the room? Was there anything out there to give away their hiding place? What were the guys doing? Were they alright? She tried to breathe more slowly and took in the narrow room, which extended the length of Cheeka's bedroom. Colourful drawings of potato-shaped people, houses and unidentifiable animals were stuck to the plywood false wall. A few had "Cheeka" written on them in large uneven capitals. Then the packet of biscuits, still in her hand, made her remember the pile of papers left out on the professor's bedroom floor. How stupid!

* * *

Downstairs, Nathan and Lyle stood shoulder-to-shoulder, backs against the walled-in under-stairs cupboard. Sounds of drawers being ransacked came from the nearby study.

'This guy's searching for something,' Nathan whispered. 'Glad I took the money.'

'This must have something to do with the creature. And what happened to the stupid dog?'

From the study came the sounds of paper tearing, plugs being pulled from sockets and wires whipping, striking wood.

'He's nicking the computer,' whispered Nathan.

Lyle jerked his thumb towards the under-stairs cupboard door and they stepped quietly around to cram themselves in beside the vacuum cleaner. From there, they heard the man grunt as he set the computer on the hall floor. Then they heard him shuffling the mail on the hall table. A door hinge squeaked.

'He must be in the living room now,' said Nathan.

Cabinet doors juddered opened and banged closed. Footsteps came into the hall again and thudded upstairs over their heads.

Nathan wiped a tickling cobweb from his face. 'Hope they're hiding properly.'

Lyle spasmed, suppressing a sneeze, and sniffed. 'Hope the creature keeps quiet.'

Creaking noises came from the upstairs hall. Then there was silence.

'He's checking out the bedrooms,' groaned Nathan. They looked at each other in the semi-darkness, holding their breath.

'We'd better move now. He's bound to check in here, if he hasn't already.'

'Head for the study – he's been there so hopefully won't be back.' They slunk across the painfully exposed hall, slipped into the study and crouched behind the desk.

Upstairs there was a thump and slithering of paper.

Lyle smacked his own forehead. 'The files – we didn't put them back under the bed. *Stupid, stupid.*'

* * *

Nikki crouched with Cheeka, staring at the false wall. She'd heard the creaking and the thud in the upstairs hall. Cheeka buried her face in Nikki's shoulder and Nikki put her arm around her. Squeaks resonated along the floorboards into their hiding place. She tensed – he was in Cheeka's room! Cheeka whimpered and pressed so close that Nikki could feel her heart beating as well as her own. She put a finger to Cheeka's lips, then flicked off the light, lest a chink escape the seal and give them away. Seconds later, a dresser drawer was wrenched open. The false wall shook. More drawers were opened and likely searched. The floor creaked again. What was he doing now? Nikki's pulse throbbed in her ears.

A man's voice roared in frustration. In Nikki's arms, Cheeka jerked with fright. They heard the little table clatter over and the pencils tinkle to the floor. Nikki and Cheeka squeezed each other tight. Finally, the floorboards told them he was leaving.

'What's happened to Einstein? Why isn't he barking?' Nikki whispered, not expecting Cheeka to answer.

'Uhh, uhh,' Cheeka grunted, and patted both Nikki's ears.

'What?'

'Uhh, uhh.' Cheeka patted Nikki's ears again. Nikki

stared unseeing into the darkness. Then wondered – was Einstein deaf?

* * *

'Sounds like he's finished trashing Cheeka's room,' Nathan whispered.

'He's furious. It must mean he's *not* found them,' said Lyle.

'Yet.'

'I say we take him down,' said Lyle. 'We can do it if we surprise him. You can use some of your moves on him.'

'But he's way bigger than us. He might even be some kind of black belt.'

Lyle was undeterred. 'I still say we go for it.'

'Maybe. Let's hide behind the door for now.'

'Yeah, and when he's busy trying to pick up the computer, we'll jump him!'

After what felt like ages, the rhythm of heavy footfalls came downstairs. Lyle began breathing loudly and flexed his fists. Nathan gripped his arm to hold him back. Through a slit at the hinge of the door they glimpsed the man dump the heap of files at the bottom of the stairs. He straightened and reached into his hip pocket, the jacket shifting to reveal a holstered gun. Lyle's eyes widened and his mouth fell open. Nathan pulled him back and silently they crept back to crouch behind the desk.

A gruff voice spoke, 'No sign of the chuman, or the professor.... Thought I saw someone at the window, but there's no one here. The mail's been stacked up but hasn't been opened for days. And the kitchen's been raided… Could've been the chuman but it's definitely not in the house right now. I checked the garage and there's only an ancient car that's probably defunct... I've found a lead or two in the house to follow… Take him out... make it look like an accident… Yeah, yeah, stop telling me my job… I know, take the chuman alive if possible.'

CHAPTER 8

The man grunted and shuffled as he struggled to carry the computer and loose files.

'We couldn't have fought bullets,' whispered Nathan, trying to control his breathing.

After a couple of minutes, a car door slammed followed by another, then an engine started up.

'He's gone,' said Lyle, wiping away cold sweat.

'Sounds like he's a hired killer.'

Lyle went into the hall. 'Yeah. Let's find Nikki and get out of here. Nikki!' he yelled.

'Shut it, Lyle…'

'But he's gone…'

'I just think we should be careful, okay? Better check the back door – Chieftain could get out,' said Nathan, heading to the kitchen.

'Cat first, Nikki second.' Lyle turned to go upstairs but stopped. 'Hey, what about that useless dog? Maybe he gave it poisoned meat.' He followed Nathan and they crunched over broken glass to peer into the utility room. The dog's body lay stretched out across his bed.

A lump formed in Nathan's throat. 'I hope he didn't suffer.'

Lyle shut the back door. 'Come on. Nikki's more important. It's only a dog.'

'Wait, I think I just saw him breathe.' Nathan stared at the Lab's chest. 'Einstein?' No response.

'Come on,' said Lyle, leaving.

The dog gave a massive snort and stretched his legs until his toes fanned out. Nathan gasped and jumped back. 'Guess he's okay.' He patted the smooth black fur.

'You know, maybe he can't hear,' suggested Lyle.

The dog got up stiffly, shook himself and yawned.

'Are you deaf, old boy, is that why you didn't bark?' asked Nathan.

'Being deaf and sleeping probably saved his life. A fat lot of good to us, though.'

'Let's see if he can find Nikki,' suggested Nathan, grabbing one of Nikki's trainers from the back door. He emptied the glass fragments and showed it to Einstein.

'Hey boy, where's Nikki?' asked Nathan.

'He's deaf, remember?'

'Maybe he can read lips.'

'Maybe he's more likely to look for the creature.'

Einstein shook himself again and, with a slight limp, headed unhurriedly out of the kitchen. They followed as he lumbered upstairs and into Cheeka's room. He sat on the clothes dumped around the dresser and gave a soft woof.

'We don't want clothes, stupid dog,' said Lyle.

Einstein woofed again and they almost fell back as the dresser slid to the side. It jammed on the strewn clothes; Nathan kicked them away. The dresser moved again and Cheeka crawled out from the little doorway.

'Oh wow, great hiding place,' said Lyle, bending to peer in.

Nikki peeked out and gazed with relief into Lyle's smiling face. 'Has he gone?' she asked.

'Yeah, well away in his car,' Lyle replied.

'He was in here. He raided the dresser – I thought he was coming through the wall. We were so scared,' she said, shakily crawling out.

'It's okay, he's definitely gone,' said Lyle.

Nikki asked, 'Was it the same man as before?'

'Must have been. He had a shaved head,' said Lyle, sticking his head into the secret room. 'Looks like a play house but –'

Nathan interrupted, 'It was purpose-built to protect her from the *danger* he was on about.' He looked at Nikki. 'That psycho said he was going to kill the professor and make it look like an accident, *and* take the chuman, dead or alive.'

'Yeah, we saw his gun,' Lyle added.

'What? He could have killed both of you,' exclaimed Nikki, her heart rate spiking again.

'It's okay, we were hiding. We just heard him speaking on his mobile,' said Lyle.

'This can't be happening. I want to get out of here right now,' she said.

'We've just got to find Chieftain, then go,' said Nathan.

Downstairs, Nikki stopped outside the study. 'Come with me a second, while I grab the address book. This is so creepy – it feels like he's still here.' She crept in and swiped the book from the desk.

They found the Siamese in the utility room sitting on the sack of dog food. He meowed and licked his lips. Nathan scooped out some dried food and put it on the floor for him and Einstein.

While they were waiting, Nikki stared through the jagged hole left in the broken back door window. Supposing something terrible had happened to Lyle – or to Nathan too, of course. She could've come out of that hiding place and found them both shot dead. She rubbed her eyes trying to erase the images.

Finally, Chieftain had had enough of crunching on the large pieces of dried dog food and let Einstein finish it off.

Before stepping outside, Nikki glanced all around. 'What if he's watching the house?' She wished that they all could be instantaneously transported back to camp.

'He's just checked the place so he'll not be back just yet,' said Nathan.

Nikki kept close to the guys as they hurried into the field opposite the house. They followed the hedges and walls closely and crouched low whenever they heard a car. No one felt like speaking until the camp came into sight.

'I can't believe this is happening,' said Nikki, as they entered the campground. 'It's like a bad dream that I can't wake up from.'

'It's real, all right, and Psycho's after the chuman and that's obviously her,' said Lyle.

'Did *he* make her?' asked Nikki.

Nathan sat at the edge of the picnic bench and lay back along it. 'No, he was on the phone to someone he's working for. Maybe they made her.'

'But why do they want her dead or live?' Nikki shivered. 'And why would he want to kill the professor? These guys must be bad so the professor must be good, don't you think?'

'Maybe,' said her cousin.

Cheeka crawled into Nikki's tent and curled up for a nap. Chieftain did the same in Nathan's tent, while Einstein rested outside.

'Come and have spaghetti and meatballs,' Nathan's dad called over the fence.

'You kids have been very quiet over dinner,' remarked Nathan's mum, as they all sat looking at adverts on the tiny caravan TV.

'We're just tired,' Nathan replied, avoiding her gaze.

'Doing what?' she asked. 'You haven't told us much at all.'

'Oh, just loads of walking about,' Nathan mumbled at the TV.

'We've explored the Earth House and Broch just near here,' offered Lyle brightly.

'Oh, you've found the Earth House, have you?' said Nathan's dad, shaking his newspaper straight. 'Some say that long ago there was a race of little people who built them as underground houses.' Nikki and the guys looked at each other.

'How about coming out with us tomorrow? We thought we'd drive up to explore the north of the island,' Nathan's mum suggested.

'Um,' Nathan began, but was saved by his dad turning up the news: '*The seventy five year old woman found shot dead in her home in Compton, Berkshire, has been named as Miss Elizabeth Ivanhoe. Police have so far been unsuccessful in tracing relatives or finding a motive.'*

Nikki and the boys exchanged looks again.

'Different name,' said Lyle.

'Yeah, *Ivanhoe* not *Ivanson*,' Nathan specified.

'What are you talking about?' asked Nathan's dad.

'Oh, nothing. We just know someone with a similar name.'

CHAPTER 9

The Inflictor hunched over his whisky, muttering like a warlock over a cauldron. The gloom in his corner of Portree's "Eagle's Nest" pub hung thick as fog. Beneath his fist lay a photograph of the professor. He flicked a penknife open and closed, open and closed - then he stabbed at the photo and dragged the blade across the neck, severing the head.

Scowling, he rubbed his stubble. Someone else must be after the chuman - but who else knew about it? Why had Brindle-Feist told him so little? Seething, he glugged back a second swallow of whisky. It burned his gullet.

Soon the alcohol would dull his anger and enable him to think logically. Someone had taken those incriminating files out of a hiding place. Surely the professor wouldn't have been so stupid as to leave them out?

He ordered another whisky. That £50,000 fee - not yet in his bank account - would pay for the conversion of his new transit van into a mobile high tech surveillance unit. Then his business would boom. He had to succeed - he had to find the professor *now*.

From his pocket, he withdrew the page he'd ripped from the phone book - a lead to follow - "Ward 3" had been hand written in the margins along with the visiting times. If the professor was in there, then tonight he'd locate the chuman – by whatever means. Even if he had to rip it off a competitor, that would be a mere inconvenience. The inevitable delay in obtaining his well earned fee would be – tolerable.

CHAPTER 10

Back at their tents, Nikki watched Cheeka slurping the spaghetti and meatballs she'd sneaked to her.

'It's really creepy about that murdered woman being called Elizabeth Ivanhoe – almost the same as Liz Ivanson,' said Nikki. 'We have to phone her.' And she opened the address book. 'Here's a *Liz*, under "L", but there's no last name. Must be her.'

Unable to find her own mobile, she used Nathan's. 'No answer. Maybe he's called her already and she's on her way.'

'Maybe she's dead. Maybe that *was* her on the news,' said Lyle.

'It's not the same name and it happened four hundred miles away,' Nikki replied, wondering if Lyle was always this pessimistic.

'So what's our next move?' asked Nathan, plucking at the grass where he lay.

'We should tell the professor about the psycho who's after Cheeka, and what he did to his house,' said Nikki. 'We can use his money for a taxi and get there in time for the seven o'clock visiting.'

'Then he can tell us what he's doing with a genetically engineered hybrid human creature in his house,' said Lyle.

Nikki shrugged. 'Maybe he won't tell us.'

Lyle raised an eyebrow. 'He'll tell us. We have *his* creature and *his* dog.'

'D'you think he collected all those papers as evidence? Like he's planning on reporting them?' Nikki wondered.

'Or blackmailing them,' suggested Lyle, giving a sideways grin.

They arrived at the hospital after only twenty minutes by taxi. 'That was so much better than the bus,' Nikki murmured, taking Cheeka's hand.

Nathan laughed. 'Hope you're not going to chuck again.' Nikki rolled her eyes and tugged at Cheeka's hood. They headed straight for Ward Three.

The nurse swished up to them, hair flaming. Nikki groaned, 'Oh no, it's her.'

'So you're here. You've a lot of explaining to do,' said the nurse.

'I don't think so,' said Nathan. 'We were just carrying out our grandfather's wishes for alternative treatment.'

'Well, his son's with him now. I suppose that's your father? I've a mind to tell him about the mud.'

Before Nikki could think or reply, Cheeka shot off into the ward. She chased her. The curtains were drawn around the bed. Nikki wasn't sure she wanted to see his visitor and caught Cheeka just before she got her hands on the curtain.

Through a gap, movement of someone in black caught her eye. She saw the back of a man's shaved head. He leaned close to the professor's ear. The professor's eyes were wide with fear.

The man's voice was rough, 'Start talking, old man – where's the chuman?'

Sharp steel glinted as a blade was pressed against the professor's neck.

Immediately, Nikki retreated, half dragging, half carrying Cheeka, who was squealing in frustration.

She said to the guys, 'Quick, we've got to get out of here. That psycho's with him. He's got a knife!'

They scuttled into the nearby and empty patients' lounge.

Fighting to keep Cheeka held against her, Nikki blurted out, 'He had a knife at the professor's neck! We should tell someone.'

Lyle's eyes flashed. 'Let's check it out.' He pushed Nathan into the hall and followed.

'Careful, it must be that same psycho,' Nikki panted.

'He never saw us at the house, so he won't recognise us,' said Nathan over his shoulder. 'Take Cheeka to the toilets and stay there till we get you.'

* * *

A newspaper trolley stood unattended in the corridor. Lyle grabbed it and whizzed it up to the professor's curtains and yanked one open.

The blade snapped into its handle, hidden in a fist.

Lyle said, 'Good afternoon sir, could I interest you in a newspaper or magazine? Oh, sorry sir, didn't mean to interrupt.'

'I was just leaving,' growled the man. He turned to the professor, 'I'll be back later – Dad.' And he left.

'Are you alright?' Lyle asked the professor, who was looking deathly white.

Nathan joined them. 'You were brilliant, Lyle.' Then he noticed the professor's shocked expression. 'Did he hurt you?'

The old man frowned, seeming not to recognise them, then his eyes widened. 'Where's Cheeka?'

Hearing the panic in the professor's voice, Nathan replied quickly, 'It's okay – Nikki's with her. They're hiding.'

'That man…' whispered the professor. 'That man's after her… keep her hidden… he's been hired by others to take her away. They're determined to find her and…' The professor's voice trailed off.

'This psycho's already been to your house looking for you and Cheeka. We were there when he broke in,' said Lyle. The professor's mouth opened in horror and Nathan pulled Lyle's arm to stop him saying any more.

'Oh my God, you were in danger.' The professor squeezed his eyes shut.

Nathan quickly continued, 'It's alright. Cheeka and Nikki hid in the secret room while we spied on him. He never saw any of us.'

'Now he's tracked me here, as you did.' He paused and looked at them. 'I can't live there any more. I'm not even safe here.'

'We should tell the police,' said Nathan.

'No, no – they'd take Cheeka away. They wouldn't understand anything about her. No one must know about her. She's not even supposed to exist.'

'But why do they want her, Professor?' Lyle asked.

'What right do they have? And who are they anyway? If you want us to help, you've got to tell us what's going on.'

'Just keep Cheeka out of sight. That's all that matters now. Thank God you found her before he did.'

'He took your computer.' Lyle looked for the professor's reaction.

'Never mind about that, as long as you're all safe. The really important information is hidden elsewhere.'

Lyle and Nathan looked at each other but neither mentioned that *they'd* taken files out and that these had been stolen too.

'We'd better go, visiting time is over,' said Nathan.

'How can I contact you?'

'You can have our mobile phone numbers,' said Nathan, and found a pen in the bedside table's drawer.

'I must tell you that Cheeka's not well. You'll have noticed that she is not like you or me – but there's no time to explain. She needs medicine, four different kinds, everyday. These help her heart, liver and kidneys function, all of which are failing slowly.' The professor breathed deeply, his eyes glistening. 'The medicine is all kept in a cupboard in the kitchen. Did she show you?'

Nathan shook his head.

'Well, she hates it. She doesn't understand why she needs it. I don't think her mud remedies could cure multiple organ failure.'

'Okay, Professor,' said Lyle, 'we'll go get it.'

'Don't take her with you and make sure you're not seen. While you're there, take the money in my desk drawer. Top left. Use it to look after Cheeka, and come to see me by taxi next time.'

The boys glanced at each other again.

'I'll be out in a couple of days. It's Cheeka's treatment you see – the doctors are astounded. The nurse was furious with the mess.'

'Talk of the devil,' said Lyle.

The nurse glared at them. 'That's enough excitement, Professor. You are doing extremely well, but it's time to rest now.'

'Remember, keep her out of sight,' he said. 'These people don't care about the law. I'm a threat to them. They would like to silence me – forever. And if they get hold of Cheeka, God only knows what they'll do to her.'

CHAPTER 11

The Inflictor gripped the steering wheel and swerved, narrowly missing a Mini.

'D'you want die? I can help you,' he shouted, bumping off the grassy verge back onto the road.

With the old man in hospital, where was that ugly chuman? He couldn't torture the information out of him with that irritating nurse patrolling. Killing him would have been easier.

But that redheaded nurse might just have given him another lead - grandchildren had visited. He snorted. She'd assumed he was their father and asked what was wrong with the littlest one - could she have meant the chuman? His clients said the professor was childless - so the kids lied - obviously hiding something - the chuman? Was the professor really stupid enough to let *kids* look after the thing and take it to visit him? With idiots like this, taking the chuman would be easy.

The nurse had asked him about his holiday with the kids - so they must be staying somewhere - probably within walking distance of the professor's house. He'd give the house another check - maybe they'd left more clues as to where they were hiding the chuman. He *would* find them, even if he had to check out every hotel, B&B and caravan on the island; even if he had to stake out the house and the hospital at visiting time.

His fists tightened on the steering wheel, his whole body now a tightly coiled spring. He was so close to finishing this job that he could almost smell the money.

CHAPTER 12

Crammed in the taxi they couldn't talk freely about all that had happened. Cheeka sat on Nikki's lap and was lulled to sleep. With Cheeka's body heat, steam seemed to rise from Nikki's damp T-shirt, soaked when Cheeka had turned the taps on full blast in the disabled loos. When they arrived at the campground, Nikki helped her onto Lyle's back.

'Lyle, you said she has organ failure. What's that? Is she going to die?' she whispered, looking at Cheeka's sleeping face squashed against his shoulder.

'Dunno. But it doesn't sound good.'

Nathan asked, 'How did that psycho find out where the professor was, anyway? Cheeka wrote *999* for Nikki, but how did *he* work it out?'

Nikki gulped, suddenly remembering the phone book left open on the professor's desk, complete with the visiting times written by *her* in the margins. It was her fault. Not wanting to admit it, she asked, 'Well, how did he find out where Cheeka lived in the first place?'

'Dunno,' said Lyle.

'We didn't find out *anything* from him, did we? We still have no idea what to do,' said Nathan.

'Or what's going on,' said Lyle. 'But we could just look after the animals for a couple more days and then we give them back and mind our own business.'

'But only if Cheeka is going to be safe,' said Nikki. 'And she's *not* an animal.' She sighed; hadn't Lyle noticed anything about Cheeka? And he really was clueless about animals. Come to think of it, she'd never actually seen him pet or talk to Chieftain or Einstein. She was going to have to teach him.

In her tent, Nikki curled up beside Cheeka, feeling as though every ounce of energy had gone from her body. She assessed each sound for possible danger and wished she was in the caravan with her aunt and uncle. That psycho had a gun and had held a knife at the professor's neck. Could they really keep Cheeka safe? And what about themselves?

Again, she woke early, wondering if she had slept much at all. This time there was no bright sun shining through the tent walls. Cheeka awoke while she was getting ready and the two crawled out into a cool, foggy morning.

Over cereal, she reminded the others, 'Not that I ever want to go there again, but we're supposed to go back to Cheeka's house to get her medicine.'

Cheeka shook her head furiously.

'Yes, we know that,' said her cousin, his hair looking more dishevelled than ever. Nikki doubted if he'd combed it since they'd arrived. Probably hadn't brushed his teeth either, she thought, wrinkling her nose. Do as little work as possible on holiday – that's him.

After a silence, she said, 'D'you think it's too early to phone that Liz person?'

'Just do it. This is an emergency,' he replied, handing her his phone.

She spoke, covering the mobile, 'I keep thinking of the psycho threatening the professor with that huge knife. You heard him say he'd keep watching the house.'

'But he *knows* Cheeka's not there and he now *knows* the professor's in hospital,' said Nathan.

Lyle scraped up his last bit of cereal. 'He might think she's being looked after somewhere. Or, because of the ransacked kitchen, he might think she's still hiding in the house.'

'I suppose we could sneak up to the house, make sure he's not around, grab the medicine and then go somewhere else – do something. Like, go down to the sea,' suggested Nathan.

'Yeah,' said Lyle. 'We're stuck baby sitting, but we don't have to stay at the camp to do it.'

'No answer,' said Nikki. 'At least if we go somewhere, your parents won't see her. Only thing is, the professor doesn't want us to take her back to the house.'

'Like I said, we'd only be dropping by. We'll make sure no one's watching,' said Nathan.

'We should go in from the back,' said Nikki, and the others agreed.

By the time the house came into sight, Nikki's stomach was knotting up and she patted Einstein for comfort. 'No sign of any cars parked anywhere. If the psycho's watching the house, where'd he be?'

'Probably somewhere that he can see the front of the

house with his binoculars. He won't have parked too near for a stakeout,' said Lyle.

'I need a drink,' said Nathan, leaving Chieftain's legs dangling over each of his shoulders while he dug out a water bottle from the pack on Lyle's back.

'I think we should cross into the fields now, and go up behind the back wall,' Nikki suggested.

They peered over the five foot high wall into the back of the property. Nikki couldn't detect any sign of movement behind the back windows. Chieftain sprang from Nathan's shoulder to walk along the wall.

'Clear,' Nathan declared, and clambered over.

'It's not a game, Nathan,' groaned, Nikki.

Cheeka hung her long fingers over the top and walked vertically up the wall until she could stand on it.

'Wait, Cheeka. Where's Einstein?' asked Nikki.

'Uhh.' Cheeka pointed towards the road, and jumped down into the garden. The Lab waddled along beside the wall.

'He'll be heading for the driveway to get in,' said Lyle, dropping the backpack into the garden. 'Can I give you a leg up?' And he cupped his hands for her to step in. So he *can* be quite considerate, she thought.

Once over the wall, she waited while Lyle heaved himself up, grunting, and fell over, landing beside her. She smiled, was he trying to be funny?

Keeping low, they quickly caught up with Nathan.

'I don't think the psycho's here,' he said.

Nikki peeked through the jagged hole in the frosted glass of the back door. 'Let's just grab the medicine and go.'

'It's not locked,' whispered Lyle, pushing it open. 'Didn't we lock it yesterday?'

'I think Cheeka did,' whispered Nikki, and Cheeka nodded, holding up the key.

Lyle stepped in and listened.

'I'm not going in,' said Nikki. 'He could be there.'

'I'll go,' said Nathan. 'You take Chieftain. Lyle, watch the hallway while I find the medicine.'

Nathan obviously didn't know which cupboard to look in but found it on the third attempt. Not knowing what to choose either, he gathered a bunch of bottles and packets and stuffed them into the bag on Lyle's back.

In Nikki's arms, Chieftain growled. 'It's alright, Chieffers, we're going now.'

The boys came out and Cheeka locked the door.

Nikki heard a bang from a window above them. Had a bird hit it? She looked up and Cheeka screamed.

The psycho was looking down at them.

Her heart thumped.

'Run,' she yelled, 'Psycho's in the house!'

Cheeka ran ahead, Einstein at her ankles, and disappeared behind the garage. Nikki and the others hurried after her.

'Hope she knows where to hide,' panted Nikki, as Cheeka opened the back door of the garage. Breathing hard, they all crammed in and Lyle dragged an old table in front of the door.

Nikki glanced around. 'Where do we hide?' The garage was over-stuffed with junk including rolls of wallpaper standing in boxes, paint tins, ropes and tools. Cheeka, shadowed by her dog, nipped around the pile of old furniture and trunks that reached the ceiling. Nikki squeezed past this mountain and glanced through the grubby little window that let in the only light. She glimpsed Cheeka climb into an ancient bubble car that faced the main doors.

'The back door's still shut, so he's not come out,' she said.

Nathan came to have a look. 'Cheeka left the key in the lock so he'll be held up opening it. Nice one.'

'He'll be here any second,' said Lyle. 'Hope he won't think we're in here.'

'The car?' suggested Nikki, and slid in beside Cheeka and Einstein. Chieftain growled and hid behind her ankles.

Lyle said, 'But it has windows, how's that a good...' Then his elbow sent a box of rusty tools clanking to the concrete floor.

'Lyle! Now he's sure to find us,' moaned Nikki.

The light dimmed and huge hands slapped the window and clawed the glass. A scarred face pressed against it, made all the more frightening by the film of dirt.

'It's him,' Nikki shrieked. 'What are we going to do?'

Cheeka leaned across Nikki and thrust her fist, dangling keys, towards Lyle. 'Uhh, uhh.'

'What?' he asked.

'Uhh!' Cheeka vigorously jingled the keys.

He snatched the keys and got into the driver's seat, blindly flinging the backpack in Nikki's face.

The back door of the garage was kicked again and again.

'She wants me to drive.' He turned the ignition. 'Do you think it actually runs?' Nothing happened.

'Lyle, you can't drive,' yelled Nikki.

'He can,' shouted Nathan, shaking the front passenger door handle. 'It won't open.'

Lyle kicked at the door. It slammed into his friend – Nathan yelled in pain and dropped into the seat.

'I learnt how to drive a tractor.' Lyle screwed up his face, as if this concentration might fire up the engine.

Start, please start, Nikki willed.

The engine choked like a strangled monster, then fell silent.

Behind them, the garage door exploded open.

CHAPTER 13

'Come on out,' yelled the psycho. 'You can't get away!'

'Lyle,' Nikki sobbed.

'Shut up,' Nathan shouted.

Over her shoulder, she saw a dark form lurch around the junk pile towards them. He was a big man and there wasn't much space for him to pass. Another tin box crashed to the ground.

Again and again, Lyle turned the ignition, but the engine only whined and coughed. 'Please,' he whispered.

Just when Nikki thought they'd be caught, the engine roared. Cheeka squealed and shook the back of Lyle's seat.

'Get out the car,' yelled the psycho, shoving and kicking stuff out of his way.

'We are go, man,' shouted Lyle. The engine revved. The gears ground metal against metal. The car jumped backwards. Furniture and trunks smashed as if dynamited. The engine screamed in their ears. Grey fumes filled the garage and seeped into the car.

'Forward, go forward,' Nikki yelled, hoping they could break the doors.

Lyle ground the gears again. Engine screaming, the Morris lunged forwards and punched open the wooden doors. One fell from its hinges. Daylight blinded them. The metal lock clanged onto the bonnet. The car made several kangaroo leaps down the drive.

'Where do I go? Where do I go?' shouted Lyle, fighting the stiff gear lever.

'Right, turn right!' Nathan shouted.

Nikki kept her eyes on the burst open garage until they had swung onto the road.

'Oh no, it's single-track. What'll I do if a car comes towards me?' said Lyle.

'Use the passing places,' said Nathan.

Nikki felt herself shaking all over. 'We might have killed him.'

'Doubt it. We just slowed him down so we could get away,' said her cousin.

'I didn't drive over him - only knocked some stuff in his way,' Lyle panted.

'What are we doing?' she cried. It was hard to speak with her mouth so dry.

'Calm down,' said Nathan. 'We did what we had to do to get away. He has a gun and a knife, remember? He could've killed us.'

She gripped the back of Nathan's seat, looking out the front. 'We've got to get out - Lyle can't drive!'

'It's okay, it's coming back to me,' Lyle shouted back.

'We're going to crash. We're all going to die!'

'We won't,' said Nathan, turning to look right at her. 'Lyle's doing great.' He glanced at Lyle. 'She's been in an accident before.'

'Oh,' said Lyle. 'I... I wonder how long we've got before Psycho gets his car.'

'Quick, turn right again,' said Nathan.

Lyle yanked the heavy steering wheel to turn abruptly onto an even narrower road that snaked through green pastures dotted with sheep and sloped down towards the grey-blue sea. A small hazy island stood between the shore and a distant lobe of Skye, just visible in the mist.

'He probably knows we took a right at the drive and might guess we'd take this first turn,' said Nathan.

'Yeah, well it's too late now,' groaned Lyle.

Nikki sniffed. 'Nathan, phone your dad, we've got to get help.'

He pressed "Dad" and waited.

'No car following us – yet,' she said, looking over her shoulder. 'I know it's black but what kind of car does Psycho have?'

'Maserati GranTurismo,' said Nathan. 'Doesn't deserve it... His phone's off. I'll try Mum. Signal's not great, though.'

Nikki imagined the Morris upside down in a ditch and Einstein and Cheeka thrown lifeless into the field. '*Please* can we just stop and get back to camp. We shouldn't go any further.'

'Just how far do you think we can go?' said Nathan, pointing to the sea... Mum's not *available*.'

'I want to stop too,' said Lyle. 'But there has to be somewhere nearby to hide.'

'It's hopeless, it's all open fields,' Nikki cried, as they rounded a sharp bend. Einstein fell on her and she shoved him off. The road went into steep decline and low stone walls crumbled along both sides, unable to contain the sheep. Two trotted out of their way.

'Oh no,' groaned Lyle.

A herd of red cows were crossing ahead. Lyle had to stop. The cows stood on the road, gazing at them. From the field, an elderly farmer called and whistled to them, but they wouldn't move.

'Should we honk them?' asked Nathan.

'Shove off,' shouted Lyle.

'Let's get out now,' said Nikki. 'Just leave the car in that passing place, it'll be alright.'

'Okay, they're moving.' Lyle took his foot off the brake. The car rolled forward under gravity.

Nikki glanced over her shoulder again. 'Oh no – I think it's him. He's coming. What are we going to do?' Her heart thudded.

'Shut up and let us think,' Nathan shouted.

Lyle grabbed the gear lever, but his foot slipped off the clutch. The car stalled.

'Lyle!' shouted Nathan.

'Come on, come on,' urged Lyle, turning the ignition. The engine roared back to life. He pressed the accelerator to the floor. Seconds later, the front left tyre slipped off the tarmac. The car shook.

Nikki covered her face – we're going to die! she thought.

Lyle swung the car back onto the road.

'He's getting closer,' she yelled. 'Where can we stop and hide?' Coming up was a group of pine trees but they were too sparse to provide cover. Ahead, the road ended in a concrete apron that fanned out onto a rocky beach where a small rusted car ferry stood disused and half beached. Their car lurched to a stop and stalled. They piled out. Einstein and Cheeka ran towards the dilapidated ferry.

Nikki yanked out the backpack. 'He knows we're here.'

Lyle snatched it from her. 'Run.'

Nathan pulled out Chieftain and shouted, 'I'd say we have about one minute.'

Nikki looked to the low rocky cliffs supporting the pasture. 'Nowhere along there. How about the boathouse?' She ran to try the shabby door.

'That's the first place he'd look,' said Nathan, struggling to keep Chieftain in his arms.

Of course, we'd be trapped and killed there, she thought, and turned to the sea. 'It's hopeless.'

Lyle hurried away from the ferry. 'No good there.' Behind him, a bank of fog moved in rapidly and enveloped the little island.

Nikki glanced over her shoulder. The black car was speeding round the bends, descending towards the beach, nearer and nearer.

'Uhh,' Cheeka shouted, shaking one of three rowing boats initially hidden from view by the rusted ferry. It was part way into the water.

'Over here,' Nikki called. She glanced over the boats. All were in bad condition, one was full of crab traps and another had a piece missing from its side.

'This one might do,' she said. 'It's got oars and I think that's just rain water in it.'

'How can we hide in that?' moaned Nathan.

'We can push out into the fog,' she said.

'Might be our only chance,' said Lyle.

On the other side of the ferry, the Maserati revved close and was suddenly silent.

'We're out of time,' said Nathan. 'Get in.'

A car door slammed.

'Keep quiet,' whispered Lyle, placing the backpack away from the puddle. He held the boat steady while Nikki lifted Cheeka in. Einstein jumped in, shaking the boat and splashing in the puddle. Nikki and Lyle got in and Nathan passed her Chieftain.

'He's coming,' she hissed, hearing the psycho's feet on the rocks.

Nathan waded in the water up to his knees to push them out further. Waves broke noisily on the dark stones, masking his splashes.

The psycho banged the boathouse door and shook it. 'You can't get away!'

At last Nathan heaved himself in, landing awkwardly and rocking the boat. Cheeka grabbed hold of the edge.

'There's nowhere to hide,' yelled the psycho.

Lyle dipped the oars and paddled to manoeuvre them so that the ferry would be between them and the beach. They listened. Waves licked hungrily at the boat. Feet hurried along the rocks.

'You're trapped, there's nowhere to go,' the psycho shouted again.

'Here, wrap Chieftain in this,' whispered Nathan, taking off his sweatshirt and handing it to Nikki. She placed the wriggling bundle between her feet.

The fog moved onto the beach and the land

disappeared. A stronger wave hit the little boat. Nikki gripped the sides tightly and hoped it wouldn't sink.

Chieftain yowled. Nikki held her breath. Had Psycho heard it? Clanging metal echoed ominously.

'He's on the ferry,' she whispered, her tongue sticking to her mouth.

'Shush,' said Nathan.

'He'll see us.' Her heart thudded. 'He could shoot us.'

Lyle gave several strong pulls to the oars, dragging them deeper into the fog. The psycho's foot falls clanked on the metal deck and she watched the flaking red paint of the ferry's rear fade into whiteness. She thought she saw the faint grey shape of a man, could he see them?

Lyle took them further and further out, working against waves that were becoming stronger with each stroke he made. Several minutes passed. Einstein settled down for a sleep.

'The fog's so thick, we can't see anything now,' she whispered.

Lyle pulled the oars up. 'I don't even know how far out I've rowed.'

The cat let out another wail and Nikki whispered, 'I wish we'd left Chieffers with your mum.'

'Too late now,' replied Nathan. 'I'll try my dad's mobile again.'

'What are we going to do?' asked Lyle, rubbing an arm. 'Do we just sit and wait, hoping that he gives up and goes away?'

'We could head for the island. Better than staying here,' said Nikki, touching the dampness that chilled her face.

'But supposing we missed it and went too far out. No one knows we're here. I vote we follow the coast,' said Nathan. 'Dad's phone's still off, and mum's not answering either. And there's almost no signal.'

'Know what?' said Lyle. 'We can't even be sure which way's back. We could have drifted or turned around.'

'You're scaring me,' cried Nikki, her stomach churning.

'Shut up. Let's just think a minute,' grumped Nathan.

She glanced at Cheeka whose eyes were closed and palms held upwards.

'How can she meditate now?'

Cheeka grunted, gripped the edge and leaned over.

'Careful, Cheeka, don't fall in,' Nikki shrieked, grabbing her arm. Then she heard laughing - but it wasn't Lyle or Nathan.

'What the hell was that?' Nathan exclaimed.

Laughing again, only nearer.

'Something's out there,' said Lyle, peering into the white fog.

'It must be the psycho. He's trying to scare us - and it's working,' whispered Nikki, shivering.

They listened. They heard it again.

'What direction did it come from?' asked Nathan.

'I'm getting pretty creeped out too. That ain't human,' Lyle whispered.

'Yeah. Sounds artificial, like a toy,' said Nathan.

Nikki imagined the psycho laughing mechanically with an artificial smile like the Joker in *Batman*. The impenetrable whiteness wasn't that different from darkness.

'We can't see, I'm scared. There's nowhere to go – no escape,' she cried.

CHAPTER 14

'Calm down,' said Nathan breathlessly. 'Look at Cheeka - she's not scared. And Chieftain's not - like he wasn't when you saw your leprechaun.'

The strange laughter was closer now. Cheeka swished her hands in the water. Right in front of her, a grey head appeared.

Nikki shrieked before realising what it was. 'A dolphin.'

It disappeared below the surface.

'Uhh.' Cheeka turned to the others, grunted and pointed to the water.

'Yes, we saw,' Nikki whispered, joy twisting with the terror that she still felt. 'But is it real? Could it be some kind of trick by the psycho?'

There was a splash at the front of the boat.

Lyle exclaimed, 'It's real enough.'

'Shush. For all we know, that psycho could be near by,' she said.

'Should we follow it?' asked Nathan. 'Sometimes they rescue people. Maybe it thinks we're lost.'

'So where's it leading us to? Psycho or safety?' asked Lyle.

'I say it's to the island,' said Nikki.

'It's an animal - we can't trust it. And how would we get back?' asked Lyle.

'We can wait until the fog goes. It'll evaporate once the sun's higher up,' she replied.

'Uhh,' said Cheeka, and scrambled to the front of the boat.

The guys switched places. Nikki guessed that Nathan would row faster than Lyle and said, 'Go slowly – don't scare him.'

'He can swim a hell of a lot faster than I can row.'

After about twenty minutes, the dolphin chattered and leapt into the air, splashing them. Nathan stopped rowing.

'I love dolphins,' Nikki whispered. 'At least he'd be able to dive away from that psycho.'

Cheeka dangled both arms over the side and the dolphin swam up to her. She put her hands on the dolphin's head and it became very still. Nikki slowly reached out, but it spied her and slipped away. 'Oh,' she groaned, then looked up. 'There's the island.' The grey image filtered through the fog and she could make out a rocky beach and cliffs.

'Good, because any further and you'd be seasick, right?' her cousin teased her. Nikki sighed – why did he have to make fun of her in front of Lyle?

Rocks scraped the bottom of the boat. The vibration disturbed Chieftain, who wailed and stood up unsteadily under the sweatshirt. Einstein sat up and looked around.

'We'll have to drag the boat ashore,' said Nathan, lifting the oars into it. 'Our trainers are soaked anyway.'

'What are those weird posts sticking out of the water at the shore?' asked Lyle.

'Oh, I think they're the ribs of a whale skeleton,' said Nikki.

Nathan laughed. 'Don't be so stupid. It's just the hull of a buried shipwreck.'

She felt hot blood rush to her cheeks – Lyle must think I'm a right idiot now. Why can't I just think before blurting things out? She looked down, pretending Chieftain needed attending.

'It'll be a great place to tie up the boat,' said Lyle. But she still couldn't look at him.

'I think the water's only a couple of feet deep,' said Nathan, slinging on the backpack. He climbed over the edge into knee-deep water. 'Right, pass me Chieftain.'

The cat projected every claw and wailed while Nikki struggled to wrap him up in the sweatshirt. Then Nathan waded to the shore and set him free.

'Do you think Psycho knows we came here?' she asked Lyle.

'Doubt it,' he answered, and jumped over, splashing her.

'Can you take Cheeka?' Hearing this, Cheeka reached her long arms towards Lyle's neck.

'Guess I've no choice,' he said, bending as Cheeka climbed to squat on his neck, gripping his shoulders with her curved feet and his head with her hands. 'This is so weird,' he muttered. Seeing Cheeka leave, Einstein jumped overboard, wildly rocking the boat. Nikki squealed and clutched the edge.

'I'll come back for you,' Lyle said, wading towards the beach.

He was smiling as he returned for her. This was

going to be fun, being carried by him, but was he really strong enough? He wasn't that much bigger than she was.

In his arms, she kept hold of the boat's rope. She concentrated on that and tried not to show that she was enjoying herself. She felt his muscles straining and knew she was a little too heavy for him. Just as they reached the breaking waves, he pretended to drop her and she shrieked.

Nathan was watching them, scowling. 'Shut up. You always act so stupid around Lyle.'

She blushed again and turned her face to the cooling breeze as soon as Lyle had gently installed her beyond the waves. Nathan was getting as bad as her younger brother. Lyle prised the rope from her fist. She heard him securing it to a post behind her. After a moment, she looked around to see Nathan with his phone to his ear and Lyle pouring water from his trainers.

Nikki stared into the fog. Einstein took an occasional gulp of salty water. The waves washed in and out, musically swishing over the stones. The boat bobbed a few feet away. Columns of mist drifted across the water like proud ghosts in procession. But she was not soothed by the peaceful atmosphere – somewhere beyond, on the main island of Skye, real evil lurked. She hugged herself, chilled by more than just the damp fog.

'That psychopath will be planning his next move,' she said quietly, and shivered.

Nathan closed his phone. 'Still no answer. The signal's even worse now.'

'We should try the pol- ' screeching overhead

interrupted her. She looked up into the bright whiteness. 'This fog's bringing out all the creepy sounds.'

'Sounds like an eagle's cry,' said Nathan. 'I wish it wasn't so foggy.'

'That fog saved our lives,' said Nikki. 'I think we should climb up to the top of the island. We could see from up there if the psycho's coming.'

'Good view of the fog,' said Nathan.

'It'll clear,' Nikki retorted. 'It always does. If we're on the beach when it lifts, then we'll be exposed.'

'Okay, let's get moving. My legs are wet and freezing,' Nathan conceded.

Almost hidden by mist, Chieftain was already ascending a narrow path. Cheeka stood between the others and the cliffs, looking up into the sky, turning around and around. Einstein sat near her, his black coat contrasting with the fog. The screeching came again. A breeze parted the fog for a moment to reveal a huge brown eagle with a pale head and neck, and white tail feathers. The wings must have spanned over two metres and at their tips the feathers splayed like fingers.

'Uhh,' Cheeka pointed to it.

'Wow,' said Nathan, 'it's a sea eagle.'

'How do you know?' asked Lyle.

'Because of its white tail.'

The huge bird tightened his circles and flew lower and lower. Cheeka was at the centre.

'Nathan, it's going to grab Cheeka,' Nikki shouted, hurrying towards her little friend.

CHAPTER 15

The Inflictor lurked, trying to steady his binoculars while the stolen boat bashed and scraped against the rocks to the east of the beach. The fog had thinned and he focussed on the chuman. What a weird thing it was, standing there on the stones with its disproportionately long arms and short legs. What right did it have to wear clothes? It was just a dumb animal.

He returned the binoculars to the field pack where he kept the other tools of his profession: rope and strong tape for immobilising people – or chumans for that matter – instruments for information extraction from even the most stubborn subjects or indeed for their final termination.

He flipped open his mobile. The signal was weak but he called his clients anyway.

'Inflictor… As you know, the first part of the job is done – all incriminating evidence has been removed from the house… Right now, I have the chuman in my sight… Speak up, I can't hear you… Yeah, I can take it alive, but it'll cost you more, as discussed. There's a complication – it's with some kids. Do you want them silenced?... True, it's unlikely they'd be believed, but I know they've taken photos on at least one mobile phone… What's that? Not an acceptable risk? Fine, but if you want these loose ends tied up – I'll need to increase my fee… Can't hear you – lost reception.'

Capturing the chuman was imminent, as was silencing those kids. Then all he had to do was to terminate the professor. The kids' pathetic voices drifted towards him. *Maybe shoot the dog first – as a warning to them and the chuman. Not quite close enough. I'll hunt them down, unseen…*

CHAPTER 16

Nikki flung her arms around Cheeka and the great bird rapidly flapped upwards, sending wisps of fog spiralling away. Cheeka broke free and climbed the cliff path with Einstein.

'Wait, Cheeka, it could get you,' Nikki yelled. 'Nathan, what do sea eagles eat?'

'Fish, mainly, but sometimes rabbits,' he arrived at her side, squinting in the reflected glare off the damp cliffs. 'Better keep Chieftain close.' The cat watched them from the trail above them all, sitting in a patch of light where the sun had evaporated a tunnel through the fog. As the cousins hurried up the steep path, Nathan glanced at her over his shoulder and said, 'He won't ask you out, you know.'

'What? Who?' Blood rushed to her cheeks, had it been so obvious? 'You mean Lyle? Why are you saying that? I don't even want to go out with anyone. Not until… anyway what makes you think I'd want to go out with *him*?'

'I'm only warning you. His family's very traditional. I think he'd only go out with a Chinese girl.'

'Shush, he's coming,' she said.

'Who made this ridiculously narrow path?' asked Lyle, arriving behind her with the backpack.

'Sheep, what else?' She smiled.

Nathan scooped up Chieftain. 'The eagle's circling us, maybe he's guarding a nest on the cliff.'

The path took them to the top of the island. Nikki glanced at the shrinking beach and felt dizzy. She stood well back from the steep face and stared across the water. The main island appeared and disappeared as fog drifted.

'Wonderful view,' remarked Lyle sarcastically.

'But the fog's clearing, just as I said, and maybe soon we can see if the psychopath's car's still there,' she said. 'Lyle, gimmie your phone. Its reception might be better than Nathan's.'

Two signal bars – might be enough. She'd memorised this number long ago. Nikki squeezed her eyes shut, *please pick up*. 'Hello? Auntie?'

'Nikki, where are you? We looked for you after breakfast to ask you to come up island with us, but you'd already gone off somewhere and you weren't answering your phones.'

'Auntie, listen – '

'I can't hear you very well, the reception's poor.'

'Auntie, where are you?'

'We drove for about an hour and a half, but we were taking our time. We'll have another barbecue tonight – '

'Auntie, there's this man chasing us. We got away but he might be waiting for us. He's a psychopath. I, I think... well, we have something he wants. You have to come and get us now and please hurry!' Nikki gave a sob. But she heard nothing. 'Auntie? Auntie are you there?' She stared at the dead phone then thrust it back at Lyle.

'D'you think she heard you?' he asked.

She sniffed. 'Maybe part of it. She'll be freaked now, if she did.'

Somewhere overhead the eagle cried and Cheeka took off in that direction. Einstein quickly wove around the grassy tufts, close to her heel.

'Cheeka,' Nikki yelled, and ran after her. Long blades of grass cruelly whipped and stabbed her legs.

Lyle thrashed past her. 'Where's she going?'

The grass gave way to scratchy clumps of heather. Nathan's terrible words about *Lyle never asking her out* echoed around in her mind. Could it be true? Maybe it was just as well, she couldn't keep secrets once he was a close friend. She fell sideways. 'Concentrate,' she muttered, rubbing away the sharp pain in her ankle.

The sea eagle cried once more. Cheeka stopped running and looked up. The eagle spiralled downwards. Nikki limped quickly over to grab her hand. 'It's too close, Cheeka. Look at the size of his beak and talons.'

Nathan stuffed Chieftain under his sweatshirt and gazed at the great bird. 'This is amazing.'

Just a few metres away, the eagle landed on strong legs dressed in brown feather trousers. He stood on an area of flat rock glistening with seepage water and folded his wings. He lifted his yellow feet up and down as if to find comfortable footing; the huge curved talons clicked on the stone. The head gracefully bowed and the beak took a drink of the fresh water that trickled into a gash in the rock. They all stood gawping, unable to move a muscle.

Einstein barked, as if he'd only just noticed the eagle

and saw it as a threat. Immediately, the enormous wings stretched out, the eagle turned away from them, displaying his wedge-shaped tail of white feathers, and launched himself powerfully into the sky. In awe, they watched the sea eagle getting smaller and smaller, fading into the haze and finally vanishing.

'Awesome,' Nathan exclaimed, 'I got some good shots on my phone.'

'That's about all the phones are good for around here,' groaned Nikki.

Cheeka let go of her hand and plonked herself down. She crossed her legs and closed her eyes.

Nikki interrupted her, 'Not now, Cheeka. We have problems to sort out.' Cheeka looked up at her, her eyes black with expanded pupils. She didn't seem to register Nikki's face – she was looking much deeper. Nikki shivered and stepped back, wondering if she was going to have some kind of fit. Cheeka reached out, took her hand and pulled her down to sit facing her.

'I wish you could talk, Cheeka, or that I could speak sign language. Then you could tell me what's going on with you.'

Cheeka lifted up her right hand and placed her palm on Nikki's forehead.

Immediately Nikki felt she'd entered a vertical wind tunnel.

CHAPTER 17

The Inflictor couldn't see the top of the island for fog, so he knew he was concealed.

'The chuman's mine and those idiots aren't leaving this island,' he muttered, freeing the kids' boat from its post. A wave filled his shoes and soaked him to the knees. He glanced up at the path taken by his prey, and growled. He couldn't directly follow them in case the vile dog detected him.

He went back to the rocky cliff that rose above the dark rocks where he'd secured his stolen boat. He climbed quickly at first but it became far steeper than he'd expected and he was no mountain goat. He clung to the rocky face like a splattered egg. There was no soil to foster any growth of grass, only slippery rock lubricated by sea spray. His wet trousers and shoes weighted his legs. His feet skidded and he swore. Think of the money, he told himself. He dug his fingers into a crack in the cliff face. They bled. His trousers tore at both knees. With every move, his field pack threatened to overbalance him and pull him to the rocks below. This would be the perfect place to stage an accident. He could see the headlines now: *Three teenagers fell to their death among jagged boulders after attempting to climb the cliffs…*

At last, he hauled himself over the top and crawled away from the precipice. He fell on his front, panting, then scrambled to his feet and forced himself onwards in the direction of the chuman. Now on high ground, and above the worst of the fog, he got out the binoculars. He focussed on some distant forms. Occasionally, he caught the sound of their voices carried on the wind.

He grunted – the end was in sight.

CHAPTER 18

Cheeka's palm was warm and firm on Nikki's forehead. A sound like rushing air filled her ears. Behind Cheeka, she could see a wall of shimmering air, like a mirage, and through it, the landscape appeared distorted and the light dimmed. Wondering if they were inside some kind of invisible dome, Nikki wanted to look around to see, but feared it would all vanish if she disconnected from Cheeka's hand.

Cheeka mumbled in her incomprehensible way and was gazing towards the sky. Nikki slowly tilted her head to look upwards. Circling a couple a metres above them and mingling with the mirage dome were several animal forms including a leaping dolphin, a soaring eagle and what she thought was a wild cat, running. They were not life sized – perhaps the size of Chieftain. The forms had volume but were not solid. They were translucent and seemed to radiate a golden light of their own. It was the most beautiful sight that Nikki had ever seen and, despite the ache developing in her neck, she didn't want to move in case it all ended. Was Cheeka communicating with them? Were they even aware of her and Cheeka? Did this mean anything or was Cheeka just doing this for fun?

Suddenly, millions of stars danced before Nikki's

eyes and her ears rang. Then everything went black. A moment later, all was whiteness and she felt weightless. Was she dead? The whiteness parted and she had a view from above, looking down on the island. She felt no fear of the height. There was the man standing far below her. He faced a cave. He spoke, but the sound was distant. He waved something. A gun. A breeze washed over her. Something darkened her view and brushed across her face. Feathers. A distant cry. An enormous bird with a hooked beak swooped down and the man disappeared behind the massive wingspan. White tail. A sea eagle soared upwards over the man. A black shape rushed from the cave. Four more figures crawled out - one figure was her.

Why can I see all this? She stretched out her hand but there was only air between her and ground below.

The eagle soared upwards, a gun dangled from its talons.

Her view followed the figures as they ran down a path, a different path from before.

She felt Cheeka's palm lift from her forehead. The vision vanished.

'What...' she began, confused.

Cheeka was pulling her up and squealing. She got to her feet, her mind whirling with the images.

'Hey guys,' shouted Nathan from somewhere below and out of sight. 'Chieftain's found some sort of cave. I can hear water trickling from inside, so it might be connected to that crack up there.'

Nikki and Cheeka peeked over the edge of the rocky surface and saw Nathan some three metres below, peering at the wall of rock that supported them. Cheeka immediately climbed over the edge and dropped down.

Nikki found an easier route and saw Chieftain slip out from a diagonal cleft in the rock. He blinked in the daylight and yowled. Nikki realised she'd just seen *that* cave, but how?

'Uhh.' Cheeka grabbed her hand and stepped through the cleft. Nikki pulled back, a waft of dank air assaulting her nostrils. Einstein brushed past her legs and slid in after Cheeka. Nikki's arm was yanked into the cave.

'I can't go in there,' she said, just as Chieftain slunk past her, growling and vanished into the cave.

'Something's scared Chieftain,' said Nathan.

Nikki shook her mind clear. Was that some kind of premonition she'd had? She dashed a look around. Her heart thudded. 'Guy's, I think the psycho's here!'

'What?' shouted Nathan.

'Where?' Lyle yelled, spinning around.

'I… I don't know. I just feel it. Let's get away,' she shook her arm free of Cheeka.

'I don't see him,' said Lyle.

'Where's the torch? We can't go in there if we can't see.' She frantically dug out the mini-torch from the backpack and shone it through the cleft. The narrow beam reflected gold off Einstein's and Chieftain's eyes and the cavern's jagged ceiling and walls gleamed wet. There'd be just enough room for them all to crouch in there.

'I don't know what to do,' she said, her mouth drying. 'Cheeka thinks the psycho's here and wants to hide in there. Maybe we should just run.'

'Oh my God, I see him,' said Nathan.

Nikki, half pulled by Cheeka and half pushed by Nathan, stumbled into the cave, her head narrowly missing the rock.

'Shove over, quick,' he demanded. She inched over, avoiding contact with the cave walls.

'Hurry, he's getting closer,' hissed Lyle, jamming in. They crouched on the dirt floor. Nikki tried to hear above the trickling water and all their breathing. The cave's musty smell like rotten lettuce almost made her gag.

'Where is he?' she asked.

'He could be here any minute. It must have been him,' answered Lyle. 'But I don't think he saw us.'

'Quiet,' whispered Nathan.

They listened for a moment. Nikki shone the torch overhead. No bugs – yet, she thought. How can I worry about creeping things when there's a psychopathic maniac out there? What an idiot. She whispered, 'I'm scared, what are we going to do?' Darkness pressed in on her. We're trapped!

'Shush. Where's the backpack?' Nathan whispered.

'Oh no!' Lyle hissed.

Nikki's heart pounded harder. 'You left it out there – that'll give us away.' She scrambled towards the cave mouth, but Lyle grabbed her and pulled her back against him. 'It's not safe out there,' he breathed in her ear.

Nikki, terrified and unable to move or speak, felt she was eight years old again – back in that crushed car, trapped in the darkness. Not now, not now, she told herself. She had shaken her dad, screaming. She felt that same panic now. His head had rolled and hung at that awful unnatural angle. She knew he was dead. Now she shifted, wanting to get out of the cave, to escape this memory, but Lyle held tight. She could still see the blood trickling from her dad's ear. She squeezed her eyes tight but the image wouldn't be banished. She thought she might be sick.

Nathan groaned. 'What are we doing in here? We could've just run for it.'

'It's too exposed out there,' Lyle explained. 'He has a gun.'

Chieftain growled. In the darkness, all held their breath. Nikki strained her eyes towards the cave mouth.

A pair of legs walked past. She heard a powerful kick at their backpack. It flew across her field of vision. The legs returned to stand a few feet in front of the cave entrance. She couldn't see his head. They were trapped between the rocky walls and a psychopathic murderer.

'Send out the chuman before I fire into the cave.' The voice was loud and rough.

Terrified, they all crouched in shocked silence. There was an ominous click.

'He's definitely got a gun,' whispered Nathan.

A deafening bang sounded and dust sprayed from the small bullet hole in the ground at the cave entrance.

CHAPTER 19

Nikki's ears rang. Her head spun. Am I really here? Is this real? Then raw terror seized her. The gun was aimed directly at her. She had to escape. But Lyle's arms firmly restrained her against his chest and she could feel his heart pounding against her back.

'I *said*, send out the chuman,' the psycho shouted. 'Or die with it!'

Her heart was beating so hard she felt she'd pass out. He'll kill us all and no one will find our bodies. No one knows we're here.

An eagle screeched. Nikki heard the sound of wings beating. Something brown swooped to block her view of the psycho. Another screech. White tail feathers flicked and then were gone.

'Ahhh!' yelled the psycho.

Einstein shoved past Nikki. Nathan shot a hand out to stop him, but he rocket launched, showering Nikki with dirt and stones, barking like a canine machine gun. Nikki peered out, fearing for his life. The dog ran directly at the psycho, his head level and lips peeled back and snarling. The psycho stepped back and lifted his field pack off.

'He's getting another weapon,' cried Nikki.

'Where's his gun?' asked Lyle.

'The eagle grabbed it,' she told them.

'What?' said Nathan.

'I definitely saw him take it.'

'Then let's go while we have a chance,' shouted Lyle, practically shoving Nikki out of the cave. She knocked her head on rock. Dazed, she stumbled and fell. Lyle squeezed out and dragged her up. She grabbed Cheeka's hand.

'Run,' shouted Nathan, with Chieftain under his arm.

The man blocked the way they'd come.

'This way,' cried Nikki. Her body exploded forward as if she was outrunning her own fear. For a moment she felt separated from her body, her spirit sprinting just ahead of her body.

'How do you know?' asked Nathan.

She flashed a look at him. His expression was desperate.

This was more than a *deja vu* feeling, she'd been shown the way. 'I just know – hurry.'

They kept running. While Einstein barked, they had a chance. Was he giving up his life for them?

'Do you think Einstein can hold him off?' asked Lyle.

'Maybe Cheeka communicated with him in the cave,' panted Nikki.

Ahead, the land stopped abruptly. Nikki halted, a rocky sheep's path dropped steeply into the fog – how could she still be afraid of heights?

Cheeka took over the lead. Being so short made her, steady on the steep descent. Nikki got behind Lyle hoping he'd block her fall if she slipped. She took her eyes off the path to look for their boat but a patch of denser fog swept across the island enveloping them in damp greyness. She couldn't even see the rocky beach below. She stumbled and looked back to the path. By the time they'd reached the beach, she couldn't hear Einstein's barks anymore.

'Hope he's still alive,' she mumbled.

'Hope this is the right beach,' said Lyle. 'I never noticed this other path before.'

Cheeka jumped off the last bit of bank and ran towards the water.

Nikki's legs were shaking from the strain of controlling her speed, and from fear. She placed hands on knees, trying to steady them.

'We've got to get away, Nikki. No time to stop,' Nathan shouted back at her. Lyle grabbed her hand and pulled her along. There was no magic in this contact – just one human being helping another, she told herself.

Cheeka reached the breaking waves first. She stood with her hand on a piece of wrecked ship protruding from its rocky grave.

'Where's the boat? There's no sign of it,' cried Nikki, frantically scanning the water. 'And the tide's gone out a bit, so it should have been grounded.' Her mind whirled – if I saw the way down in the vision, why didn't I see the boat too? It ended too soon…

'Well, this is definitely the same beach,' said Nathan, banging his fist on the post. 'You didn't tie it properly, Lyle.'

'Yes, I did,' he retorted. 'That evil sod must have untied it.'

'Ahh,' groaned Nathan, grabbing his head.

'What about *his* boat?' suggested Nikki. 'He must have had one, where's that?'

'Can't be far. He must have been here to untie ours,' said Nathan.

'We've got to find it before he gets to it,' said Nikki.

'Let's split up,' said Lyle, heading towards rocks that flanked the beach.

Cheeka took her hand as they sprinted off after Lyle.

'No sign of it from up here,' panted Lyle from a high point on the rocks.

After another moment, they heard Nathan shout from within the fog, 'Found it.' And they rushed across the stony beach to join him.

'It's the one that was full of crab traps,' said Nikki, spotting the remaining one under the seat.

Lyle untied it while Nathan popped in a wailing Chieftain, and steadied it for Cheeka and Nikki.

'What about Einstein?' Nikki searched the boys' faces but they avoided eye contact, their expressions dark and serious.

'We can't just leave him. The psycho might kill him.' Her voice quavered.

'What do you suggest we do?' shouted Nathan. 'We'll all be killed if we go back.'

'I think even the professor would have sacrificed the dog for Cheeka,' said Lyle quietly.

Nikki wiped a tear away, staring into the patches of fog that drifted across the beach.

Nathan used an oar to push away from the rocks, and said, 'Keep looking. He probably has another gun.' He stripped off his sweatshirt and threw it at

Nikki. She wrapped up Chieftain in it.

'D'you think Einstein could swim as far as the main island?' she asked hopefully. No one answered. All was quiet except for the paddling and Nathan's regular breathing as he rowed as hard as he could. The water became quite choppy, making him work harder. Salty water splashed onto Nikki's face. She felt numb. How could all this be real? A psychopath after them? In her mind the gunshot exploded again. It *was* all true.

'We must be out of gunshot range, don't you think?' asked Nathan, panting. 'And the island's almost hidden in fog now.'

'Not unless he has a sniper rifle in his bag,' said Lyle.

'I'd better keep going then,' said Nathan.

'Can you imagine what any of our parents would say if they knew what happened to us today?' asked Nikki.

'I don't even want to think about that,' said Lyle.

What would my dad have thought of this? She could hardly remember his living face, only the photographs. Where was he now? Heaven? Was he her guardian angel? Is that how they escaped? Life – *death* – it was so confusing.

Cheeka leaned against Nikki. Nikki put her arm around her, glad of the distraction. She wished she knew more about her. She reflected on the strange experience they'd shared. Was it some kind of telepathy? She must be a very special kind of being. Were those animal spirits connected with the dolphin and sea eagle they'd seen today? She'd seen the way to escape. It saved their lives.

Cheeka closed her eyes and slithered down to lay her head on Nikki's lap.

Nikki said quietly, 'You know, at first Cheeka seemed really weird and unnatural. But now it looks like she has some special talents that maybe no one else has. D'you think that's why these people want her back so bad?'

'What talents?' asked Lyle.

'Well, I'm sure she helped my head, and the professor seemed much better after her treatment,' she paused, looking to Nathan for help. He said nothing. 'She also seems to have a link with animals, like the dolphin and eagle and probably Einstein.'

'What are you talking about?' asked Lyle.

'Forget it,' she said, thinking – now he's convinced I'm an idiot, and no way am I telling them about the trance Cheeka shared with me.

Nathan stopped rowing, his T-shirt wet with sweat and fog. 'They want her dead *or* alive, remember? So they probably don't even care if she has any talents. They probably don't even know anything about her. She's just an experiment.'

Nikki shivered, who could want to hurt Cheeka?

The boys switched places and Lyle took the oars and rowed at a slower pace.

Nikki looked at Cheeka and noticed that the skin under her eyes had darkened. Was she ill or just tired? Then she remembered. 'Guys, we've lost Cheeka's medicine. It was in the backpack. We'll have to go back to the house to get more.' So much for promising to look after her properly, she thought.

Nathan scowled at her.

'It's not my fault,' said Nikki huffily.

'The drinks were in there as well,' Nathan moaned.

Nikki's stomach rumbled. She was empty but not hungry. She dragged her free hand in the water and peered through the fog. 'There's the old broken ferry and the shore.'

Lyle rowed until the bottom of the boat scraped the rocks. They all clambered out, not caring about refilling their trainers with water. Nikki longed to be back at the camp, back with her aunt and uncle, back to safety. But what about poor Einstein? She felt a lump rise in her throat.

As if he'd read her thoughts, Nathan said, 'We'll find a way to get the dog. Maybe an anonymous phone call to the police, or something.'

'Yes,' Nikki replied, feeling better, 'we can do that. We need to keep off the…' Nikki almost choked on her words. A middle-aged man and woman, both in dark suits, approached them. They looked stiff and unfriendly. The others stopped with her and she took Cheeka's hand. Chieftain growled from the sweatshirt bundle under Nathan's arm – always a sign of danger.

'Who are they?' she whispered, her stomach knotting.

Simultaneously the two adults reached into their inner jacket pockets, brought out ID cards and flipped them open.

It was the man who spoke, 'This is Inspector Smyth and I'm Detective Inspector West. You are all under arrest for car theft and kidnapping.'

CHAPTER 20

'You do not have to say anything, but it may harm your defence if you fail to mention, when questioned, something which you may later rely on in court. Anything you do say may be given in evidence,' DI West recited.

Nikki tightened her grip on Cheeka's hand. 'Wait a minute, we're being chased by a psycho, and we were actually wanting to contact you for help.'

'Oh yes? And where is this psychopath now?' asked West, looking around and sneering at her.

'You must come with us back to the station in Portree for questioning,' said Inspector Smyth, studying Cheeka.

'I don't understand. Who reported us?' Lyle voiced what was also in Nikki's mind.

'Professor Ivanson, of course,' answered Inspector Smyth.

'What?' said Nathan. 'We're *helping* him.'

'You took his car, and his…' West paused, eyeing Cheeka.

'Once you listen about the psycho, then you'll understand why we had to take it,' said Lyle.

'To the car, please. Now,' said DI West.

Confused, Nikki muttered, 'Why would he report us? This doesn't make any sense at all.'

'I thought he trusted us,' whispered Nathan.

'Maybe he's nuts,' Lyle replied.

They were herded towards the deep blue Mazda. An unmarked police car, she supposed.

Nikki whispered, 'Once they know the truth, they'll help us.'

'Hurry up,' said DI West.

'We... we've actually left a dog on the island,' Nikki stammered.

'Then he'll have to swim back,' said Inspector Smyth.

'But it's too far and he's old.'

'Then he can wait until low tide and walk.'

Was it only an island at high tide? Nikki hoped it was true.

'Get in,' demanded Smyth, holding a back door open. Nikki and Lyle slid in with Cheeka on Nikki's lap. No one guided their heads in as she'd seen done on TV.

'There's no seatbelt for Cheeka,' said Nikki. Smyth glared at her.

'Leave the cat,' Inspector West said firmly.

Nathan stepped back, 'I am not going without him.'

'Look kid, do you want to add resisting arrest to your growing criminal record? Now dump the animal and get in the car.'

Nathan didn't move. From the car Nikki saw his eyes flashing.

'If you bring the cat, it'll only get put down,' West shouted.

'Would the police really do that?' Nikki whispered, hoping that they were bluffing.

'Get out of the car,' Nathan shouted to the others, 'we're not going anywhere.'

Before Nikki could think what to do, DI West had roughly gripped Nathan by the arm and Inspector Smyth was prising Chieftain off his neck.

'This can't be happening,' muttered Nikki.

Chieftain, like his master, wasn't giving up without a fight. Twisting to bite her, he transformed into a nightmare of hissing, growling and slashing claws, but she grabbed him by the scruff of his neck and his limbs went limp. She tossed him, like a piece of rubbish, into some long grass.

Nathan was shoved roughly into the car beside Nikki and the door slammed. Tears of pure rage trickled over his tightly clenched cheeks. His balled fists rested on his lap. Nikki knew his mind was back there with Chieftain. Also feeling desperately worried for *both* animals, she touched his arm for their mutual comfort.

DI West started up the car and quickly pulled away sending out a spray of grit.

'Look,' Nikki tried to sound brave, 'we haven't kidnapped Cheeka. We're looking after her for the professor. He's in hospital. What's going to happen to her?'

'Hey kid, we ask the questions, not you,' said the DI West.

'Excuse me, but Cheeka needs her medicine. She's got serious medical problems. It's all at the professor's house. It's only a couple of minutes away so we could stop and get it.'

'What's wrong with her?' asked the woman.

'Her liver and kidneys don't work properly,' said Lyle.

The police glanced at each other. West muttered, 'Could be a problem.'

'Okay, we'll stop by to collect the medicine,' said DI West.

After a few minutes, they swung into the drive. They had no trouble finding the place. Nikki supposed that Professor Ivanson must have told them *exactly* where he lived.

'Alright, you've got two minutes,' said the DI. 'Get out.'

'I think the key might still be in the back door,' said Nikki, helping Cheeka out the car.

There was something about these cops that didn't seem right to her – like the rough way they handled Nathan and Chieftain. But maybe they were just mean – some were, weren't they? Cheeka clung to her leg, whimpering. It was hard to walk like that. On the way to the back door, her mind raced. Maybe they could give them the slip, somehow.

'In,' said West, ushering them through the back door. Now Nikki noticed his foreign accent – but 'West' wasn't a foreign name. Doesn't mean he's bad, though.

Nikki watched Nathan step over the broken glass. Why didn't the cops say anything about the obvious break in? Or were they going to be accused of that too?

Nikki dropped to one knee. 'I just dropped an earring.' She bent down to pretend to look among the stones. 'Hurry Lyle, help me.' She didn't even have pierced ears – yet.

'Huh?' He squatted beside her.

'Leave it,' growled West.

Nikki whispered, 'We've got to get away from these people.'

'I know, I know,' he breathed. 'Did you notice? That's a rental car – they must be *fake* cops.'

'We have to warn Nathan,' she said under her breath.

'Get up,' yelled West.

Nikki and Lyle quickly joined Nathan and at the far end of the kitchen. Lyle whispered, 'You two get to the secret room. I'll distract them, then join you.' Nathan looked at him questioningly. 'Just do it,' Lyle hissed.

'Where's the medicine?' demanded Smyth.

Nikki flung open the kitchen cupboard and grabbed a handful of packets and bottles.

Smyth put her hand out for the medicine. 'Let me see those.' She inspected the label of one bottle. 'Captopril – that's for heart failure. Let me see the rest.' Turning to West, she said, 'Christoff, looks like it has multiple organ problems.'

'This isn't good,' he muttered, as she dumped the packets in his hands. He frowned and handed the lot back to Nikki. 'Bring them.' And under his breath he muttered to Smyth, 'Not the healthy specimen we were hoping for then.'

They weren't talking like cops. They sounded more like doctors. Lyle was right, they're fakes and they're trying to get Cheeka. We've got to get away, thought Nikki.

'Don't worry about the chu – about what's her name,'

Inspector Smyth told Nikki. 'She'll be well looked after. Bring her over to me.' But Cheeka squealed and hid behind Nikki. No wonder she doesn't like you, witch.

'I'd better get Cheeka's bag and a few of her toys and clothes from upstairs. If she doesn't have her stuff she'll get very difficult to handle. Believe me – I know,' Nikki lied.

'I'll come with you,' said Inspector Smyth, reaching for Cheeka's hand. But Cheeka growled showing her large canine teeth.

'I think she needs to say goodbye to her room in private,' said Nikki.

'You have one minute.'

As Nikki led Cheeka away she heard Lyle trying to distract them.

'Could we get some water?' he asked. 'After all that rowing we're pretty thirsty.'

'Hurry up,' said the woman, checking her watch. She opened Cheeka's medicine cupboard and read more packet labels.

'I'm going to the loo,' said Nathan, heading down the hallway.

'Make it quick,' said DI West, following him. He watched him go upstairs.

Lyle took his time finding glasses and handed one to Smyth, who immediately put it down. Lyle brought another to DI West who was nosing about the hall.

'I'll just take Nikki her water,' said Lyle, and hurried up the stairs, slopping water as he went.

Smyth joined DI West, and said, 'I don't like this. They've all separated. Make sure they don't leave the house.' She took his glass and dumped it on the hall table.

'Hurry,' said Nikki from the doorway of Cheeka's secret room. The little light was on. Lyle handed her the water and squeezed in. The dresser slid smoothly into place, closing and concealing their door.

Nikki told him, 'We tied two sheets together and hung them out the window, so they'll think we've escaped. And Nathan chucked my shoes out onto the grass so it'll look like I lost them running to the back wall.' She looked at the medicine in her lap, then spotted a hideous old handbag obviously used for dressing up games, and crammed in the packets and bottles.

'They'll come looking for us any second,' said Lyle.

'Shush, they're coming up,' said Nathan, switching off the light.

West shouted, 'Get down here now! We're leaving.'

Through the false wall, Nikki heard the muffled sounds of their footsteps and frantic voices. Then she felt the vibrations of the floorboards as one of them, she guessed the man, came into Cheeka's room. The footfalls stopped. She hoped it was in front of the window – was their set up convincing? From there he shouted for the woman and she hurried in.

They heard the man's voice. 'Damn it, they've escaped. Looks like they've gone over the back wall.'

'Well, you go after them,' said the woman. 'I can't – not in these shoes.'

'Then use those trainers left on the grass,' commanded the man.

'If the Inflictor had done his job properly we wouldn't be going through this ridiculous charade.' The shrill voice left the room.

'The kids have seen us now, so they definitely need taking care of,' said the man.

The sounds died away and they heard the back door slam and a few more pieces of glass shatter on the floor.

'So the psycho's called *the Inflictor*,' Lyle whispered. 'What kind of a sick name is that?'

'They said, *take care of us*. I suppose that means *kill us*?' asked Nikki.

'Obviously,' said Nathan. 'He's probably still on the island, so we have plenty of time to get away.'

Raised voices came from outside.

'They'll be looking over the wall,' said Nathan.

Cheeka's stomach rumbled. She put the light back on and opened a toy chest. She lifted out bottles of water, melting chocolate bars and bags of nuts and raisins.

'That's great, Cheeka,' said Lyle. They opened bottles and drank.

'It's so stuffy in here,' said Nathan, wiping his mouth.

'Shush, they're coming back,' said Nikki. A moment later, she heard someone creeping about the room. Were they about to be discovered? She heard glugging and sloshing sounds, like liquid being emptied from a large container. Then the footfalls faded away. A couple of moments later, two car doors slammed and a car started up.

'Should we wait a few minutes before looking out?' Nathan asked. 'Just in case it's a trick.'

'Not too much longer, it's getting really hot in here,' said Lyle.

They quickly ate the sticky chocolate. Cheeka, as usual, fitted a whole bar into her mouth at once.

Nikki stopped chewing, 'What's that roaring noise?'

'That's not a car. It's closer,' said Nathan.

Glass smashed in Cheeka's room.

Nikki's heart pounded. 'Why's it getting so hot in here? Cheeka open the door!'

Cheeka opened it halfway but the roaring sound knocked her backwards onto Nikki. Immediately, immense heat invaded their little space. Through a bright glow, Nikki saw enormous flames consuming Cheeka's bed, table, carpet, curtains – everything. The pretty room had been transformed into a blazing furnace. Black smoke billowed across the ceiling and out of the broken windows. The open bedroom door and its frame were on fire and it looked like the hall was ablaze too.

'We can't get out,' she shouted to the boys over the deafening roar.

Cheeka scrambled up and pulled all her weight on the closing mechanism, but it wouldn't budge. Nikki lunged forwards to help her. Behind her the guys were shouting. She pulled at the metal door handle but it was too hot to touch. She tugged at the side of the little door. Over her shoulder one of the boys was shaking out water bottles onto the carpet in front of their doorway.

Glass exploded in other rooms – the whole house must be on fire.

Nathan's hands appeared on the wood beside hers.

They tugged and tugged together, but to no avail.

The dresser burst into flames and fell apart, spilling burning clothes.

Nikki's face and eyes baked and acrid fumes stung her nostrils. This was the beginning of the end for them. Her heart pounded and the hot air scorched her throat.

A wall of fire moved towards them, blackening the carpet. Flames licked around their door. In a few seconds their hands would burn. There's no hope, she thought. Any minute now her hair and clothes could catch fire, then she'd die screaming in agony.

'How are we going to get out?' shouted Nathan.

The air rushed out of the secret room to feed the fire and the bedroom ceiling caved in and noisily crashed onto the burning furniture. Nikki screamed and the heat burned her lungs.

Hands gripped her upper arms and pulled her back and just where she'd been, the rug burst into flames.

Choking on poisonous smoke and cornered by fire, they huddled at the back of the secret room. The fire roared in their ears and they couldn't hear anything else.

We're about to die a horrible death!

CHAPTER 21

Nikki crouched and coughed, clutching to her chest the handbag containing Cheeka's medicine.

'Pull your shirts over your noses,' yelled Lyle, as they crammed together watching the fire devour the secret door. But Cheeka stood in front of them and pulled at their shirts, grunting in frustration. Then she shoved Nikki and Lyle aside and slid up a piece of plywood revealing the outer masonry wall across a gap of about a foot. A narrow metal ladder was pinned against the wall.

Their light went out as the electricity cut. Seconds later, Cheeka clicked on a little battery operated light stuck to the wall and nimbly climbed down the ladder.

'A way out,' said Lyle.

'You next, Nikki,' said Nathan.

But she couldn't seem to move. Smoke swirled around her, strangling her so that she couldn't breathe. Someone yanked the bag from her and dropped it down the opening. Then she felt her own shirt being pulled up and over her nose and mouth.

'There's a window. Come on down.' Nathan called from below.

It was Lyle helping her. He turned her to face the

opening and pushed her legs to hang over. Coughing in her ear, he tried to tell her what to do.

Nathan shouted up to her, 'Nikki, just grab the ladder and come down.'

She found herself descending. Light from below penetrated the smoke. The bottom, at last. Fresh cool air was drawn in from the window. Cheeka was already outside.

'Hurry up, Lyle – we're running out of time,' shouted Nathan.

Nikki climbed out the window and Cheeka took her hand, making her run to the back lawn. The boys followed, coughing and gasping. They all collapsed on the soft cool grass, sucking in fresh air, and watched the bright flames consume the wooden window frames. Pieces of broken glass tinkled down.

'It's amazing how fast a house can go up,' said Lyle, coughing. He found Nikki's shoe nearby and tossed it to her.

Nathan said, 'I'm really worried about Chieftain – but maybe if he'd been here – I just don't want to think about it. I have to go back for him.'

'Einstein too,' Nikki added.

Nathan flipped open his mobile and dialled.

'What are you doing?' asked Nikki, not thinking clearly. She heard her own voice shaking and realised she was shivering all over.

'Fire brigade. Eden House, Portree Road, Balicraig, Isle of Skye.' He paused, listening. 'No, no one's hurt… Hurry.' And he hung up. 'Reception's okay here.'

'We'd better tell the professor,' said Lyle.

'Can't we just let the fire brigade or police tell him?' asked Nathan.

'Lyle's right,' said Nikki, coughing. Her voice still hadn't recovered. 'We should tell him right away so he knows Cheeka's alright. I'll do it. Gimme the phone.'

'How come you never have yours?' he asked.

'I think I left it in the house the first time. So it's melting now.' She squinted at the washed-out phone number written on her hand and wondered if the professor was capable of picking up.

'Professor, it's Nikki... yes, yes I'm fine. Yes – ' she paused to cough, 'Cheeka's fine too. I'm afraid I have bad news. They've – they've set fire to your house.' She paused to let him take it in. 'Are you still there, Professor?'

She had to reassure him again that everyone was alright.

'Then, really my only loss is my book collection.' His voice cracked.

'Yes, I'm afraid everything's gone.' She started crying and quickly handed the phone to Nathan.

'Uh, this is Nathan, Nikki's cousin.'

She tried to listen to Nathan's side of the conversation, but now couldn't stop crying. It was so embarrassing. Lyle put his arm around her and squeezed. This only made her worse. It was as if a dam had broken. So much had happened in such a short time. And she was so tired. Cheeka stroked her face and made purring noises.

Walking away from them, Nathan continued, 'We called the fire brigade... no, we're not waiting for them...Yes, okay... but why can't we speak to the police?… Do you want us to phone your sister for you? We found her number… No, okay… Okay, we'll find it. …Okay, right, bye.'

He snapped his phone shut and turned back to them. 'What's the matter?'

'That's what's the matter,' she cried, pointing at the house. 'We nearly got killed and the poor professor's lost everything.'

'No one's hurt – that's all he cares about. And he's got all the information about the embryo experiments scanned onto a CD that he's hidden in the greenhouse. He wants us to get it. Let's do it now before something else happens.'

Lyle helped Nikki up and walked her over to the greenhouse where Nathan was throttling geraniums and ripping them from their pots.

'The professor said it's in a pot, under a plant,' he explained.

'Let's help,' Lyle suggested to Nikki. It was a distraction for her. She didn't like this further destruction of the professor's belongings, but this was an emergency.

A few evicted geraniums later, Nathan announced, 'Found it,' shaking the potting soil from a plastic zip lock bag protecting the CD. 'Let's get out of here now, before the firemen and police get here. They'll want to question us.'

'Why can't we tell the police now?' Nikki sniffed. 'The real police, I mean.'

'D'you want Cheeka to be taken away? We'll be back at the camp soon. My parents will be back and we can look at the CD and then tell them. But first, I'm going back to find Chieftain. You guys don't need to come.'

'Hey, we don't go anywhere alone – not after all this,' said Lyle.

Sirens sounded in the distance and rapidly got louder. They all dropped over the back wall and set off on the kilometre long walk across the gently undulating sheep pastures that sloped towards the sea. They walked diagonally from the house to the beach, cutting off much of the distance they had travelled earlier on the twisting road.

'They could be watching out for us around here. They might guess we'd go back for the animals,' said Nikki.

'At least the Inflictor is probably still on the island,' said Nathan.

'Since we can't even see the road with this hilly ground, that means no one can see us from the road either,' said Lyle.

They walked in silence for a bit then Lyle said, 'Dinner as soon as we get back. Right, Nathan?'

'I can't think about food or sleep until I've found Chieftain,' Nathan muttered, and sped up to walk ahead of them.

'Don't worry, we'll find him,' Nikki called after him. Cheeka grunted as if in agreement, dragging the handbag behind her.

Nikki thought again about what Nathan had said to her earlier on the island.

'Lyle, um, is your family very traditional?' she asked, trying to sound natural.

'What do you mean?'

'Well, Chinese traditions and things. Like *feng shui*, I guess.'

'Not my parents. My grandparents? Yes. When my cousin had a *boy* baby, they had a whole roasted pig for a celebration.'

She tried asking a couple more questions about Chinese traditions. It all sounded very interesting but she couldn't bring herself to ask outright if he could go out with a non-Chinese girl. She would have to be patient and enjoy his friendship. They were only thirteen after all. And they were lucky to still be alive. She smoothed her hair and felt some melted strands at the front – if he gets to know me better, maybe he won't mind me being a freak.

'Can't be much further,' said Lyle. 'The fog's almost gone. I can see the island.' He looked at his mobile and frowned. 'Hmm, no service.'

A car engine sounded and Nikki's heart thudded. She saw Nathan crouch down and grabbed Lyle's arm, pulling him down.

'That sounds near. Could be him leaving the beach. There's nowhere to hide,' she said.

'It's okay, we're not in view of the road so he can't see us. Whoever it is, is going pretty fast.'

They continued on and Nikki looked ahead. 'Look, there's the beach and the psycho's car's definitely gone. That was close, but he'll be searching for us. Wish we were back at the camp.'

'I hope that was someone nicking his car, that would slow him up. Wonder what he did to the dog.'

Nikki moaned. 'I really want him to be alright.'

Ahead of them, Nathan ran onto the road and yelled, 'No, oh no!'

Nikki and Lyle ran to catch up. Nikki gasped. She saw a slim grey body lying at the side of the road. Her mouth went dry.

CHAPTER 22

In a low powerful gear, the Inflictor's Maserati sped up and away from the beach, scattering sheep left and right. Sea water drained from his clothes and trickled over the black leather seat. He rounded a bend and thump! A large woolly object flew in an arc ahead of him. The wheels screamed to a halt. He jumped out to inspect the bumper and swiped some wool away from the dent. A wave of rage swept through him like wildfire. He spun around to face the motionless sheep. He channelled his fury through his legs and gave the animal a massive kick off the road. It lay on its back in a shallow ditch, legs pointing heavenwards.

The Inflictor smacked the roof of his car, then movement on the road below caught his eye. It could be his prey. He clawed inside his bag for the binoculars. Focussing them, he saw it was the idiots and the chuman. He flung the binoculars back into the bag and snatched his second gun from the glove compartment. He flicked the safety catch back and aimed first at the girl's head, then at each of the boy's. He inhaled through clenched teeth. Too far away – he'd have to reverse down the track. He tossed the gun onto the passenger seat and dropped back behind the wheel. He turned on the ignition and twisted his neck to see the track behind him.

Then there was another engine noise and the Inflictor whipped around just in time to see a white van fill his windscreen. He saw the driver's wide-eyed horror. Brakes screeched.

Bang!

The Maserati GranTurismo, still in neutral, leapt backwards. The Inflictor's neck was thrown back, then forward as his car came to a sudden stop, tilted upwards – back wheels in a ditch. He gripped his neck, watching two men get out the van. His anger was fuelled – they'd just made him lose the chuman, again. And they'd damaged his car – and neck. He glanced at the gun that had been knocked to the floor.

'You alright, Mister?' asked one man, approaching his car door.

The Inflictor flung it open, with rage building until the veins of his neck and forehead stood out from his reddening skin.

'You're all wet,' said the other man, frowning.

The Inflictor glared at him, breathing through flared nostrils.

The first man turned back to the van and said, 'I'll get our insurance details for you.'

'I don't want your stupid details, just get my car out of the freaking ditch,' the Inflictor yelled at them.

CHAPTER 23

Nathan turned away. 'It's alright, it's just a squirrel.'

Cheeka reached out to touch it, but Nikki pulled her back. 'It's too late, Cheeka.' The fright had left Nikki with a feeling of dread. Their luck was bound to run out soon.

'We'd better keep off the road,' said Lyle, and led them back into the pasture.

'Yeah, the fake cops could be waiting for us.' Nathan added.

Nikki shivered. 'I keep getting that creepy feeling of being watched.'

'That's just because of what I said, and because we were exposed on the road,' Nathan replied, but glanced around all the same.

There was a bang in the distance, away up the road somewhere.

'What was that?' Nikki asked, looking across the rolling pastures. She couldn't see much of the road but could make out the white roof of a parked van.

'It's nothing,' said Lyle, following her gaze. 'Probably just its engine back firing.'

As they neared the sea, the stone wall gave way to the gorse hedge where Chieftain had been tossed into the long grass. The cousins called softly for him, peering under the hedge. No answer. Supposing he tried to find his way back to the camp and got lost, Nikki worried.

Cheeka stomped off across some muddy grass mashed up by hooves.

'Wait, Cheeka, we have to stick together,' Nikki called, but she ignored her. Nikki hurried after her, wondering if sometimes Cheeka just *knew* things. Cheeka squatted down and looked under the hedge beyond which the land dropped a metre to the beach.

'Uhh.' She looked back at Nikki and grinned.

Chieftain's narrow face with bright blue eyes and out-sized ears popped out from under the spiky branches. Nathan and Nikki both called him and he tiptoed towards them. She was so relieved, she could have cried. Nathan scooped him up and buried his face in his fur before draping him around his neck. Chieftain was purring so loudly that his whisker pads were vibrating.

'Let's check the beach just in case Einstein made it back,' she said, peering towards the island through the thin, wind ravaged gorse bushes.

'The tide's really far out,' said Nathan.

'It was already on its way out when we took the boat,' said Lyle. 'It takes about six hours and – '

'Forget the geography lesson, Lyle,' said Nathan.

'It might be quite shallow. Wish we had binoculars,' said Nikki.

'We can't wait around too long,' said Lyle, watching the road. 'The psycho probably killed him anyway.'

'Lyle!' shouted Nikki.

'Well, you have to face it. We left him there with a psychopathic murderer.'

'Wait a minute. It *could* be a seal, but I think it's Einstein swimming,' said Nathan.

Nikki squinted to see. Nathan had such good eyes, eagle-eyes, his mum said. Moments later, she could make out a black head bobbing in the water. 'I see it.'

'It *is* him,' exclaimed Nathan, after a few more minutes. 'A seal wouldn't travel in a straight line towards the shore, and it would keep on diving. Nikki, take Chieftain.' He ran the many metres distance across the stony beach, calling the dog.

'He might as well shout: *here we are come and get us*,' complained Lyle, eyeing the road behind them.

'He keeps forgetting the dog's deaf, too.'

'Maybe seeing Nathan will make him swim harder.'

Soon the black Labrador was breaking through the waves and wading towards Nathan.

'He must be exhausted and starving,' she said.

'So are we,' said Lyle.

Einstein collapsed on the rocky beach without shaking himself dry. Nathan had to tug at the lose skin on his neck to persuade him to get up again. He limped slowly over the long stretch of stones and Nathan had to tug at him every few steps to keep him moving.

Nikki patted his wet body when they arrived. 'Who's such a clever boy? I don't think he can walk yet, we'll have to let him rest.'

'Better not,' said Lyle, looking around again. 'They'll be hunting down their chuman and then they'll kill us.'

Nathan hung Chieftain around his neck. 'Lyle's right, let's go.'

They headed back to the camp through fields and

pastures, only crossing roads as they bisected the landscape. Einstein, head hanging low, limped beside Cheeka. She kept one hand resting on his damp shoulders, and from the other she swung her handbag.

'My legs ache and I don't think I could run fast enough if they chased,' moaned Nikki. 'And Einstein doesn't look up to a fight.'

'Well, I'm starving,' complained Nathan.

'I stink of sweat and burnt hair,' said Lyle, and made the others laugh a little.

'I miss my mum,' admitted Nikki.

'I miss my sofa,' said Nathan.

'I miss my normal life,' Lyle added.

They arrived at the camp totally drained of energy.

'It's nearly four. Your mum and dad might be back now,' said Nikki.

'I'll go see, and I suppose I could turn the barbecue on ready. Could you feed Chieftain?'

Nikki opened tins of cat food for Chieftain and Einstein.

'Uhh,' said Cheeka, pointing to the cat food.

'No, Cheeka, it's disgusting.' But Cheeka picked up a new tin and thrust it in her face. Sighing, Nikki opened it and gave her a spoon. Cheeka scraped the tin clean, wiped it out with her finger and licked it, then, yawning widely, she crawled into the tent. Nikki covered her up with the sleeping bag and invited Einstein to come in too, her faith in him as a guard dog somewhat restored. Zipping them in, she heard Nathan's voice behind her. 'They've just got back and Dad's starting the barbecue. Let's flake out in the caravan, and Chieftain's coming with us.'

'Your mum obviously didn't hear me on the phone then.' Nikki sighed, wondering what was the best thing to do now.

She hugged Auntie Lynne – an extra long one.

'Nikki, your hair smells of smoke, where have you been?' she asked.

Nathan rescued her. 'Nikki, Dad wants to know what you want to eat.'

She went to the cramped bathroom and sniffed her hair. Auntie was right about the smoke. She found some nail scissors in the mirrored cabinet and cut off the melted bits.

After their meal, she slouched with the others, watching TV. Chieftain lay on Nathan's lap. It felt so safe that she wished she could stay the night, in fact, she really longed for her own home and, like Lyle, to have her normal life back.

Nathan's mobile phone rang. Nikki jumped.

'Hello?' said Nathan, then handed her the phone. 'It's your mum.'

'Hi, Mum. I'm so glad you called,' said Nikki, taking the phone outside. 'I... I really miss you.' She found herself caressing the phone with her thumb.

'Nikki, is anything wrong?' asked her mum. Nikki fought back tears and assured her everything was fine.

'Nikki, aren't you missing something? Aren't you wondering why I'm calling you on Nathan's phone?'

'Uh?' Nikki hesitated, not wanting to say she'd left her phone in a burning house.

'Have you been into Portree?'

'Uh?' Nikki felt flustered. They hadn't put together

a story to tell the parents if needed.

'On a bus?'

'Yes, actually we did go there yesterday.'

'Well, you left your phone on the bus. A man found it. He said he'd drop it off in McKay's Convenience Store. He says it's the only shop in the village. Nikki, you must be more careful.'

'How do you know all this?'

'Obviously he turned on your phone, went to menu, picked "*mum*" and called me to ask what to do with it. It was very nice of him. I obviously didn't say where you were staying but asked him if he would drop it off at a shop in Portree or preferably Balicraig.'

'Sorry, Mum. We'll pick it up tomorrow.' They spoke on for a few more minutes, then she slowly closed the phone. Never before had her mum felt so far away.

Inside the caravan, she looked at Auntie Lynne. She was sitting right there but she felt far away too. She told the others about her phone and Uncle Pete insisted on driving her to pick it up, saying he wanted to get some milk and a paper anyway.

'Nikki,' said Lyle quietly. 'Is there any chance it could be a trick?'

CHAPTER 24

The Inflictor watched McKay's Convenience Store from across the road in his dented Maserati. He took a slug from the beer bottle bought while dropping off the mobile phone he'd found on the mantelpiece in the professor's study.

'I'm closing in,' he muttered, cleaning his fingernails with the blade of a camping knife. The inscription on the handle read: *Nathan Adams*. Then he stabbed the knife into the kids' wet backpack which lay on the seat beside him.

He'd guessed the girl would want to pick up her phone immediately – they cost money; they stored images. He looked at his own phone to which he'd already sent the girl's chuman pictures. He lingered on one, the chuman had formed some kind of monkey grin. But what was happiness? He couldn't understand it. The closest he got to it was a sense of satisfaction. Perhaps there was something missing within himself, an invisible something, but just as significant as a limb.

Of course the girl wouldn't come *alone* to the shop that evening, so he'd simply follow her to see where she was hiding the chuman.

He watched a man and a girl enter the shop. Could that be her? He wasn't sure, they all looked so similar.

Moments later, the same girl exited the shop, smiling, eyes on her mobile. It *was* her, and she never once glanced in his direction. Had she forgotten the danger she was in? People this stupid didn't deserve to live. He watched them pull off down the road before he started the car. He followed at a distance and observed them turn onto a lane towards woodland.

The small sign read: *Balicraig campground.*

CHAPTER 25

In the car, Nikki flipped her mobile phone over and over in her hand, hoping that Cheeka was still asleep in the tent. As soon as they got back to the caravan, she hurried in to get the guys. Seeing her, Nathan threw the tea towel at Lyle and asked his dad if they could borrow his laptop.

'Sure, but the battery's low. And make sure you don't leave it outside.'

Minutes later, they huddled around the screen in the boys' tent.

'Here goes,' said Nathan, feeding in the CD. 'Look at all those folders. He's got loads of evidence on these guys who made Cheeka.'

Nikki read out the file names, 'Chimp-human hybrid embryo images; Chimp-human hybridized DNA; Chimp pregnancy records; McBraidy at work…'

'Where do we start?' asked Lyle.

'How about that one,' said Nikki, pointing to one named *Open Me first*.

'It's a video file,' said Nathan, adjusting the sound. An image flickered and filled the screen. It was the professor sitting behind his desk. He spoke to the poorly angled camera: *'If you are watching this then I may be dead already, or my life in danger. Saved onto this CD are a variety of scanned letters, laboratory notes and photographs documenting a series of illegal and immoral experiments with human-animal hybrid cloned embryos that were carried out at the Institute for the Advancement of Human Health. At the time when I was collecting this evidence, the experiments culminated in the birth of a chuman: a part human, part chimpanzee baby that by the time of this recording, had reached the age of four years. It is very likely that this project continues, as it began, in secret. Please take this CD to the Government Home Office or to the police.'* The message ended.

'So he *does* want to tell the police. Should we call them or go hand it in?' asked Lyle.

'He's not dead,' said Nikki.

Lyle stared at her. 'But his life is in danger. Our lives are in danger.'

'He only asked us to pick up the CD, he didn't say to hand it in – so we should ask first,' said Nathan.

'Open that folder called *Incriminating letters,*' Lyle suggested.

'Yeah, this must tell us something,' said Nathan. 'It's a scanned copy of a letter: *Dear Dr McBraidy, I am very pleased that you have agreed to go ahead with the chuman project. The rejection of the project licence application by the Government Home Office need not deter us. These small minded people are incapable of seeing the bigger picture as you and I do. Do not involve Professor Ivanhoe; he has too many scruples. Shortly, we shall transfer funds to the agreed amount, £500,000, to cover research expenses. A further £500,000 shall be transferred to your personal account after the successful completion of the project. Best regards, Christoff Brindle-Feist.*'

'So maybe Professor Ivanson wasn't involved with her creation *at all,*' Lyle surmised.

'Guys, didn't you notice?' asked Nikki. 'The letter said *Ivanhoe,* not *Ivanson.* Are they two different people or did he change his name?'

'Dunno. If he was hiding the chuman from them, maybe he changed his name a bit,' said Nathan.

'And isn't it bit of a strange coincidence that the murdered old lady in England was called Ivanhoe?' Nikki pointed out. 'I don't think it's a common name.'

'Can't see a connection between an old lady and a chuman experiment,' said Lyle. 'Could this Brindle-Feist weirdo with the big bank account be one of the fake cops? The woman called the man *Christoff,* remember?'

'If Professor Ivanson or Ivanhoe, whoever, wasn't involved, then why does he have Cheeka?' asked Nathan.

'Like Nikki said the other day, maybe he rescued her. Remember that project application thing to the government? It didn't have his name on it,' Lyle reasoned.

'I'm kind of hoping the professor is a good guy,' said Nathan.

'That's the low battery warning flashing,' said Lyle. 'Better charge it up in the caravan. We can do more in the morning.'

'I really think we should tell your parents now,' said Nikki. 'We've done our best; now we need help.'

Nathan replied, 'Let's tell them first thing in the morning. They can't do anything tonight and we're safe for now.'

'We'll be in deep trouble, but at least it'll be over,' said Lyle.

Yawning, Nikki crawled into her tent. Einstein no longer smelled of dog after his long swim, but she still didn't fancy sharing the same air and gently pushed him out. Feeling heavy with fatigue, she snuggled down next to the sleeping Cheeka. But as soon as she closed her eyes, she could see the flames devouring Cheeka's room and hear the roar.

Nikki woke suddenly. It was dark. What was that noise? Her heart thudded. She turned to see, right by her head, a sharp blade slice down the back of her tent.

CHAPTER 26

Nikki quickly rolled away just as a pair of arms thrust through the cut. She knew it was the psycho – he mustn't get Cheeka. Frantically, she dug at the cover to find her. A black-gloved hand clawed for Cheeka's shoulder and woke her.

Another fist aimed a long needle above her body. He was going to drug her –or kill her! Just missing the stabbing syringe, she grabbed Cheeka by the hips and pulled. She had to save her. Cheeka shrieked.

The fist brought the syringe down. Nikki screamed, yanking Cheeka to the side. The syringe jabbed through the mattress.

'Help me! Help me!' Nikki yelled, and thumped the man's arm as hard as she could. He made no sound but left the syringe swaying in the mattress. Nikki thumped him again but it was as if his arms were made of iron.

Now both gloved hands clamped onto Cheeka's shoulders and dragged her towards the slashed opening. Nikki pulled Cheeka's little hips. Cheeka's eyes were wide with terror and she twisted to bite the fists. Her head disappeared through the opening. Nikki felt her body slide through her hands. She was loosing her. The leggings were slipping down. Cheeka kicked and kicked. Nikki grappled to get hold of her ankles. A foot struck Nikki's chin, making her jaw snap to bite her tongue.

'Let her go, you psycho!' yelled Nikki, spraying blood and pulling Cheeka's ankles.

Outside, Nathan's voice shouted and beams of torchlight flashed around.

Suddenly, Nikki fell backwards with Cheeka's release. She gathered her up and the two clung to one another crying.

'What the hell's going on?' demanded Nathan, sounding afraid and fighting to unzip her tent.

Nikki was shaking, her voice trembled, 'He... he tried to grab her.'

Both boys peered in at her, leaning over the sleeping Einstein.

'How? Where did he go?' asked Nathan.

'What took you so long? I knew we should have told your mum and dad,' she cried, angry as well as scared. He should have listened to her before.

'How did... Oh my God,' exclaimed Lyle, as his torchlight caught the slashed opening. 'Are you alright?'

'Someone's coming,' said Nathan. 'Actually, a few people are coming.'

'Hello, over there. Is everything alright?' said a man in pyjamas.

'Uh, yes... thanks. My friend just had a nightmare,' said Lyle, and waved. 'Everything's fine now, thanks.' But she heard the fear in his voice.

'Some nightmare,' said the man, leaving, as another marched up.

'Oh no, it's our grouchy neighbour,' said Nathan.

'I'll be speaking to your parents tomorrow,' he snapped, probably waking more people than Nikki did.

'Oh shove off,' Nathan muttered.

Cheeka was crying into Nikki's shoulder.

'He tried to inject her,' Nikki sobbed. 'He almost had her.'

'Man, look at the size of that syringe,' said Lyle.

'How did you stop him?' asked Nathan.

Lyle answered for her, 'He obviously took off when you screamed and woke everybody up. You did really well.' He patted her arm.

'How did he find us?' cried Nikki. 'He'll be back. He knows where we are – it's not safe here anymore. I'm scared, let's go to the caravan now.'

Nathan briefly touched her shoulder, 'Come to our tent, Lyle and I will take turns keeping watch until morning.'

'No, I want to go to the caravan *now*.'

'Let's not freak them out tonight. First thing in the morning, I promise.'

'That guy's supposed to kill us, are you forgetting?' she cried.

'He's just failed so he won't try that again tonight,' said Lyle, looking towards the eerie trees. 'We'll keep watch, and if there's any sign of him, we'll wake the whole camp.'

Nikki helped Cheeka to step over Einstein.

'Useless dog,' said Lyle, and give him a shove with his bare foot.

'He can't help being deaf.' Nikki sniffed.

'Hey, should he be this sleepy?' asked Nathan, lifting

the dog's unresponsive head. His tongue hung out, covered in dirt. 'I know he's tired but…'

'He's dead,' cried Nikki, kneeling and gently stroking him. Her tears dropped onto his lifeless body. 'That psycho's killed him. He probably injected him first.'

Nathan put his head on his chest. After a moment he said, 'No, his heart's beating, but really slowly. And he's breathing. He must have been drugged. You lot get in our tent and I'll drag him over.' Nathan slipped his hands under the dog's shoulders and heaved him right into his tent.

Nikki lay between the drugged dog and poor, trembling Cheeka. In her mind she kept reliving the abduction attempt. The rims of her widened eyes were burning from not blinking. She listened to every breath of wind and rustle of leaves. She was terrified to stay there, but decided it would be too dangerous to cross the darkness to the caravan.

It was seven a.m. and Nikki sat in the tent chewing a breakfast bar but could hardly swallow the dry crumbs. She felt so tired. How could Nathan think that she would sleep after what had happened? Beside her, Cheeka sat cross-legged on a sleeping bag, cleaning a stone with Nathan's toothbrush. She was so innocent; once danger passed she seemed to act all normal again.

Outside, Einstein had recovered during the night and was keeping watch with the guys. In her head, she rehearsed her explanation for Auntie Lynne and Uncle Pete. Then a mobile phone rang making her drop her bar. She sighed, found it under a pillow and passed it out to Nathan.

'It's the professor,' said Nathan, covering the mouthpiece. 'He's getting out today and wants to collect Cheeka.'

She overheard him giving directions on how to find their tent. Tears stung her eyes, and she could feel last night's fear that Cheeka could have been taken or killed.

She heard Lyle say, 'I suppose we might not have to tell your parents after all, unless they see him.'

'Doesn't matter, it's all over now, thank God. He's taking her back,' Nathan replied.

It was late morning when a taxi rolled slowly towards their camp and creaked to a halt. Nikki watched the driver help Professor Ivanson out. She approached him, glancing over her shoulder towards the caravan.

'Hello, hello, how are you all?' he said, paying the driver.

Cheeka, hearing his voice, rushed out of the tent.

'Careful, Cheeka, don't knock him over,' warned Nikki. He had a stick to help him walk to their picnic table.

'Cheeka, have you been a good girl? Have you given Nikki and her friends any trouble?' Cheeka was so excited to see him that she didn't know whether to sit on his lap or jump up and down. She tried to do both.

Nikki shuddered – supposing I hadn't woken up last night and the psycho *had* got her? she thought.

Einstein bounded over like a young dog and Cheeka put her arms around him. Then she stood up in front of the professor. Her expression darkened and her heavy frown shielded her eyes from connection with the others.

'What's the matter, Cheeka?' he asked. But Cheeka pouted and turned away. 'She's mad at me.' Then, Cheeka whirled around to face him again. Her eyes flashed and her fists burst into a torrent of signing.

The professor translated aloud, *'Why did you go away? No one to look after us. Not enough food. Had to go out to look for something to eat. They found me.'* Cheeka quickly gestured to the others. The professor continued translating. *'They looked after us, they fed us. You promised that you'd protect me but you didn't. We were in danger. And where were you?* – Slow down, I can't read so fast, – *I never had any friends. You wouldn't let me. I said I needed friends, but you didn't listen. But they are my friends. I love them. I want to stay with them.* – Oh Cheeka, can you ever forgive me?'

Cheeka snorted loudly and went to play with Einstein. The professor stared after her with glistening eyes and rested his chin in his good hand. Nikki felt embarrassed to be present while Cheeka laid into him. The questions she'd so wanted to ask had flown from of her mind. She remembered sitting on her own dad's knee and him telling her that he'd always protect her. Well, he couldn't, could he? Neither could the professor protect Cheeka.

Lyle quickly broke the awkward silence, commenting on the obvious: 'You look much better, Professor.'

'Yes, yes, you see,' he tried to use his right arm, 'this arm is getting stronger and I can walk now. It's Cheeka

I have to thank. And I thank you all for keeping her safe. She's all I have left. Come here, Cheeka. Let me say thank you.' But she ignored him.

Nikki anxiously looked around them and over to the woods. 'Actually, Professor, she's not safe here anymore. That man tried to grab her last night.'

'What, here?' The professor's expression was horrified. He looked around nervously. 'I'd better not stay long.'

'He's called the Inflictor and, like you said before, he's working for others,' said Lyle.

'Yeah, and yesterday, all three were trying to get Cheeka from us,' Nikki continued.

'You mean you were chased. I'm so sorry that I've put you all in this danger. You must tell me all that's happened,' said the professor.

Missing out the bit about driving his car, they told him about the island, the fake cops, and their narrow escape from his burning house.

'That was a brilliant secret room you made. We'd all be dead if it wasn't for the escape route at the back,' said Lyle.

'I trained her to hide there if anyone came to the house. It was also part of my plan if anything should happen to me. She's signed to me that she'd dialled 999 when I collapsed, unlocked the front door and then hid until I'd been collected. She was supposed to call my sister and play her my recorded message – but she didn't. If she had, then maybe…' He paused. 'Anyway, can you describe these phoney police?'

Nikki answered him. 'They looked about the same

age as our parents. Forties I suppose.' She tried to describe their hair colour and heights. The guys were of no help.

'They must have used fake names, but the woman did call the man Christoff – a name we saw in your files,' said Lyle.

'Must have been Brindle-Feist and McBraidy,' muttered the professor, staring at the table. 'You've seen the files then? You have the CD?'

Nathan retrieved it from his tent. 'We looked at it on my dad's laptop. We just wanted to know more about – well, all of this.'

'I would've done the same. And yes, I do owe you an explanation for Cheeka and the trouble we're in.'

'The Inflictor was meant to take Cheeka and to *take care of us* too...'

'Kill us,' Lyle interjected. 'As well as you, Professor.'

'This is what I've been hiding from for four years, ever since I've had Cheeka. They must have hired this 'Inflictor' to – well, to do just as you've said. You must leave Skye, it's not safe.'

'How do you think they found you?' asked Nikki.

The professor took a deep breath and rested his head in his good hand. 'It was through my sister, Liz. She was found in her house a few days ago, murdered. They – or rather, the Inflictor – likely tortured her first to get my address.' The professor's eyes moistened again.

Nikki bit her lip. No wonder she didn't answer the phone, she was dead.

'Did you change your name from Ivan*hoe* to

Ivan*son*?' she asked. The professor nodded. 'We heard on the radio and TV, the other day, that an old lady called Elizabeth Ivanhoe was murdered in her house. Was that your sister?'

'Liz Ivanhoe, yes. Well deduced.' The professor fished out a handkerchief to blow his nose. Nikki wished that she hadn't asked. He continued, 'Of course, we'd always kept in touch. I couldn't just cut off all links with my world. She would send clothes and toys for Cheeka. I wanted her to come and live with us, but she had her own life in England.'

'How did you get Cheeka in the first place?' asked Nikki.

CHAPTER 27

The professor squeezed his eyes shut and rubbed his eyebrows. 'For many years I worked as a geneticist at the Institute for the Advancement of human Health.'

'Is a geneticist someone who studies genes?' asked Nikki, glancing at Lyle, wanting to show him that she knew.

'That's right. McBraidy's an embryologist. I suspected she was illegally genetically engineering chimpanzee-human hybrid embryos. Christoff Brindle-Feist put up the money for her research. I collected evidence whenever I could. I *had* planned to expose them as soon as I had enough proof. I didn't know she'd actually implanted embryos into a female chimp until there was a successful birth. I recognised the baby at once for what she was.'

'You mean Cheeka?' asked Nikki, her eyes wide.

'Yes. I was working late one night. There was screaming in the chimp house. The technician, who was supposed to be looking after the mother, was out cold, blind drunk. The mother was alone and having difficulty in the birth. It was terrible. I had to deliver her baby, although I know nothing of such matters. The delivery was very difficult because the baby's head was so big.'

Nikki wasn't sure she wanted to hear any more and found herself putting her hands over her ears.

'Was that because it was part human?' asked Lyle.

'Yes. The bigger brain meant a bigger head. Fortunately, the baby was fine. But, to my horror, it wasn't over – there was another one. Sadly, this one was born dead. He couldn't have survived. He was horribly deformed. The mother went into shock with loss of blood. I couldn't save her.'

The professor took another nervous look around. 'There I was in the lab, holding a newborn chuman wrapped in a towel. The mother was dead. What was I to do? She should never have been produced in the first place. I had no idea what McBraidy planned to do with the chumans, but it was unlikely to be good for them. In a moment of madness, I took the surviving baby home. McBraidy just assumed that the mother died giving birth to a single stillborn, deformed baby. I took early retirement and never returned. We've been hiding on Skye ever since.'

'And you raised Cheeka by yourself?' asked Nikki, softly.

'Yes. My wife died five years ago. We had no children. What did I know about babies? It was a real struggle.' He chuckled. 'Especially keeping her secret. Somehow they must have discovered that there'd been a surviving twin. Maybe they took a closer look at a scan. It wouldn't have been difficult for them to work out that I'd taken her.'

'And now they want her back,' said Lyle.

'Of course. To them, she's *their* creation. She's the ultimate evidence of their illegal work. If I ever reveal her existence, they'll be jailed.'

'Then why haven't you reported them?' asked Nikki.

'If I had, Cheeka would likely have been put down immediately – destroyed. I couldn't let that happen.'

'You definitely did the right thing,' said Nikki, smiling at Cheeka. 'Professor, how ill is she?'

He rubbed his beard with the good hand. 'Humans and chimps don't have the same number of chromosomes so she has some problems with her physiology. Do you understand?' Nikki nodded, sort of getting the gist. 'She's four now and I don't know how much longer she'll live. Perhaps less than a year. I just want her to be happy and well for as long as possible.'

'Oh,' said Nikki. 'I'm afraid I've still not given her any medicine. But we saved some of it from the fire.'

'I'll give it to her today.'

'Have you seen your house?' Nikki asked.

'Yes, I stopped by on the way here, there's nothing left. The police said it was arson. My car was stolen too. It was a 1965 Morris 1000. Quite valuable.'

Nikki and the others exchanged looks.

Lyle confessed. 'Actually, Professor, your car's okay.' He explained what happened and that it was probably still down at the beach close to his house. 'In fact, here are the keys.' He pulled them out of his pocket.

The professor laughed. 'Well I'm pleased that I still have my car. Lyle, you know you weren't insured to drive it? And do you actually have a licence?'

'Uhh – no.'

'How old are you?'

'Uh, thirteen. We're all thirteen.'

'Thirteen! So young, and I let you have the responsibility of protecting Cheeka.' He paused. 'Where are your parents?'

Nathan pointed. 'Mine are staying in a caravan over there.'

'Oh, and do they know what you've been up to these last few days?'

'No, not really, not at all, actually.'

'What are you going to do now?' Lyle changed the subject.

'Well, Cheeka and I will have to find somewhere to stay while we look for a new home. And we'll continue to hide for the rest of Cheeka's life. Right now, I must speak to your parents, Nathan, to explain that you need to get away from Skye.'

They agreed to tell Nathan's parents that they'd helped look after Cheeka and Einstein and that there were some dangerous people on Skye who might come to their campsite, looking for Cheeka.

The professor shuffled along with his stick and Nikki wondered if she should run ahead to borrow her aunt's wheelchair for him. At last she knocked on the caravan door. She watched Uncle Pete's and Auntie Lynne's puzzled faces while she made the introduction. They all sat outside at their picnic table. Nathan's mum sat in her wheelchair and mentioned to the professor about her MS. The professor was quite charming but Cheeka stared constantly at Auntie Lynne. Lynne stared back. Nikki guessed her aunt would be too polite to ask what was wrong with her.

Cheeka got up, strode confidently up to Lynne and

clambered onto her lap. Lynne, looking quite shocked, couldn't lean back any further.

'Don't worry, Auntie, she's really friendly. She thinks she can help you. She helped my head and she helped Professor Ivanson get better.'

'Uhh.' Cheeka wriggled to get comfortable and placed her hands on Lynne's head. She stroked her hair and Auntie Lynne's shoulders dropped a little and she closed her eyes. Then Cheeka seemed to grasp her head firmly and began her mumbling. Lynne quivered beneath her touch.

After a couple of minutes, Cheeka released her and the professor lifted her down. 'I don't want to raise your hopes too high, but Cheeka does seem to have some healing powers. I believe she *did* help me.'

Nikki peered at her aunt. Was she going to get up and walk? But why was there a tear trickling down her cheek? 'Are you alright, Auntie?'

'Yes, yes. That was the strangest but most beautiful experience I've ever had. Even if I never get any better, I feel a peace that I haven't felt for years.' She looked at her husband and smiled.

'I'm usually sceptical,' said her husband, shuffling his feet. 'But there are still many things beyond our knowledge.'

The professor took Uncle Pete's elbow and led him away from them. Nikki edged closer to eavesdrop.

'What, leave here? But why? We've not finished our holiday.' Uncle Pete almost shouted. The professor spoke too quietly for Nikki to hear. Again, Nathan's dad raised his voice. 'What do you mean the kids are in danger?'

Nikki groaned, sure that her own explanation would have gone down better. After a few minutes, the professor, holding Cheeka's hand and with Einstein at his heel, came over to say goodbye.

Uncle Pete followed, herding them. 'I'm taking them to where he left his car.'

Cheeka hugged Lynne, who said, 'I'm feeling stronger already.'

Nikki put the bag containing Cheeka's medicine on the back seat, then decided to come for the ride. She sat in the middle with one arm around Cheeka and the other around Einstein. Her eyes filled with tears. She'd only known Cheeka a few days but it felt like years – she loved her. She didn't want her to get ill and die. She wished they lived near each other. She'd miss Einstein too.

To her relief, the professor was able to direct her uncle to the beach and didn't mention Lyle driving the car.

'Strange place to leave your car, Professor,' muttered Uncle Pete.

Perhaps the professor pretended not to hear; he said, 'Nikki, I've had to move with the times. I've bought myself a mobile phone in Portree.'

Nikki promptly made sure that they had each other's numbers on their phones.

'You've been very kind,' said the professor. 'Cheeka and I will always be grateful to you for looking after her and Einstein.'

Uncle Pete waited until he'd seen the professor's car move off before starting his car. Then the sky darkened and a crack of thunder preceded torrential rainfall. The windshield wipers could barely keep up. Nikki hardly noticed.

'When we get back,' her uncle said, 'you're all going to tell us exactly what's been going on these last three days.' They drove the few minutes back to the campground in silence. The rain stopped as quickly as it had begun. The path to the tents was now dotted with puddles and the stream swollen with run off. But everything about the camp looked ordinary and safe and not the sort of place you'd expect to find a psychopathic killer.

Nikki felt completely flat. 'I miss Cheeka already,' she said, scrambling into the guys' tent. 'I know she loves the professor but she has no friends.'

'I don't miss any of the hassle we had looking after her,' said Nathan.

'I'm not sure what the professor told your dad, but he wants us to tell him the rest. They might want to leave right away after that. He seems pretty angry, but at least it's over and we'll be safe now. I'm just going to the loo. We can go when I get back.'

'Be quick. The weirdos won't know the professor's taken Cheeka. They could still come looking for her,' said Lyle.

'I know, but she's not with me and there are other people around now,' she replied.

The air was heavy and humid with evaporating moisture. Chieftain slipped out with her. He headed to the stream, shaking each paw in turn in a fruitless attempt to remove the water. He crouched and stared at the far bank and there, Nikki saw a water rat enter its home. Suddenly, Chieftain slunk back into the tent. Had he growled? She wasn't sure. She spun around. Small children played around a nearby tent. A camper's kettle whistled. Everything seemed so ordinary - surely she could manage the short walk to the toilets on her own? She scanned the group of trees where the toilets had been erected. They were too sparse and their trunks too narrow for anyone to hide there. As she set off, she began to dread the upcoming confrontation with her uncle. How would he and Auntie Lynne react? Her mum would eventually find out too. There would be a major row and grounding once she returned home.

Sunlight escaped between clouds and wisps of steam rose from the damp path in front of her. She felt more wary as the path entered the trees. Dead leaves rustled and she dashed a look, only to see a grey squirrel shoot up the trunk of a Scots pine.

A mother and child came out of the loos.

It's obviously safe. Maybe I'm just creeped out because of all that's happened, she thought.

Her phone rang out in her pocket, sending her heart into a tumble. She stopped to get it out, telling herself to calm down. She stared at the unknown number.

'H - hello?'

No answer.

Suddenly, a body slammed into her from behind, knocking her breath out. For a second she thought it was a runner who hadn't seen her. Then from behind, a powerful arm immobilised her and pulled her body tightly against his. She wriggled, but he gripped her so tightly that she could hardly breathe, let alone scream. He was dragging her away with her legs kicking uselessly. Her nose and mouth were compressed under a strong hand holding a cloth wet with something cold that stung her nose and eyes. She shook her head and opened her mouth trying to bite, but her mouth filled with cloth and chemicals and he pulled her head back tight against his chest. She couldn't see, but she knew it was *him,* the psycho – the Inflictor. This must be it – he really did have her this time – there was no escape, no one to help.

Fumes scorched her airways and her eyes watered. Blackness pulsed through her blood vessels to her head. Her strength and senses abandoned her. Nothingness.

CHAPTER 28

Nikki opened her eyes and tried to focus. Her head hurt. She lay on a dirty wooden floor. Light seeped between the wooden boards of a wall that she faced. It must be a shed, but where? She could hear the sea close by, so maybe a boathouse? Her mouth was taped over. She tried to move but her hands were bound behind her and her ankles were taped together. She flipped around to face into her prison.

Immediately, her eyes settled upon an imposing man glowering at her from a deckchair in front of the only door. He was dressed in black and wore a black beanie hat. The Inflictor.

Her heart thudded and the room seemed to spin. What did he want with her? Where was Cheeka, was she still safe? Where were the guys, did he have them somewhere too? Was she alone with him? Her blood turned cold.

The Inflictor's thumb clicked on a mobile phone. Why would he have a pink one? Then she realised it was hers. Green light from the little screen illuminated his bristly chin and nostrils, casting sinister shadows up his face. A scar crossed his left cheek, likely gouged by a knife. He sneered at her, teeth glinting in a black mouth. All this time he'd said nothing.

She screamed but behind the tape the sound was like a squealing pig. She looked for anything that could help her. Her eyes flashed from a pile of blue nylon netting to a heap of old crab traps and then she spotted a pair of oars leaning against the opposite wall. How could she get one of them? She couldn't move anyway. It was hopeless – there was obviously no escape.

She breathed hard, but through her nose, her heart pounding against her breastbone. She tried to think but her head throbbed – he must have used chloroform to knock her out. She thought of him handling her, and taping her up while she was unconscious. She'd never felt so repulsed in her life. He'd touched her skin – he'd picked her up. She might have even breathed in his breath. She felt nauseous. What about her hair? It was still there, it felt okay, but she couldn't touch it to make sure. She struggled but couldn't separate her wrists or ankles. She kicked and wriggled and groaned behind the tape.

'Professor Ivanhoe, I presume,' the Inflictor spoke gruffly into her phone. He used the professor's real name. This was obviously met with silence. Nikki froze, holding her breath. What was going on now?

'I have the girl. I'll make it simple. You hand over the chuman and the girl lives. You know how this sort of negotiation works. If you contact the police – the girl dies. If you contact anyone at all – the girl dies. Wait for my instructions.' The phone snapped shut.

His cold, harsh words still hung in the air. Her panic grew and she felt sick. It was hard to breathe and her nostrils flared as she forced the air in and out of her lungs. Multiple thoughts ran through her mind. She tried to grab one and concentrate, but couldn't. Will I ever see my mum again? He might just kill me whatever happens – I've seen his face. I wish I'd been nicer to everyone. What will happen to Cheeka? What can the professor do? He's too weak to fight. Would he really give Cheeka up for me? He could just run with her and let me die.

The Inflictor watched her.

She couldn't judge how much time had passed when the Inflictor finally picked up the mobile again. She felt suspended in time. What was he going to say? What would the professor do? It seemed an age before the professor answered.

'Professor, you've had enough time to consider my offer. Are you going to comply with the exchange?... Good. You wouldn't want the death of a young girl on your hands now, would you?... I know an interesting place to meet. It's called Lovers' Leap. Do you know it?... Yes, the cliff at the sea. You have precisely one hour. Come alone. If not – well, you know the rest.' He thrust the phone into his pocket.

He yanked her up, faster than she could stabilize her legs and nearly dislocating her elbow. She squealed in pain. With his other arm, he whacked the deckchair aside with undue force sending it clattering to the far wall. He kicked the door open and it smashed onto the outside wall, shaking the shed and bouncing back to hit Nikki as he pulled her out onto a rocky beach. The bright daylight hurt her eyes and she wondered if this was the last day of her life. The professor wouldn't be able to give up Cheeka to save her but guiltily she hoped he would. She imagined her mum's grieving face. She hoped it'd be quick, that he wouldn't torture her.

Unable to walk with taped ankles, her trainers scraped over mounds of stinking seaweed and jagged rocks as he dragged her. He threw open the car boot and with one movement he scooped her up and dumped her onto the tools that lay there. Just before he slammed her into darkness, she caught sight of a computer and the stack of files she'd found under the professor's floorboards.

Her eyelids stretched open but the darkness was thick as tar. Her nostrils filled with the smell of petrol, oil and dirt. But there was something else… evil.

CHAPTER 29

The engine started up and the car lurched. Nikki's body rolled.

He'll kill me, she thought, and dump my body in some ditch or the sea.

The car wobbled as if the road was pitted. She tried to hold her head up to stop the constant bashing. She was already bruised from the first journey when she was unconscious. Eventually the car moved onto a smoother road and increased its speed. She was thrown from side to side as the car rounded bends. What if he crashed? This time she might die, or be left to die in the boot. But this time it wasn't her fault - or was it?

The car swung round. She rolled and viciously cracked the side of her head on something metal. A wave of nausea passed over her and her stomach heaved.

Oh no, my mouth's taped. She couldn't suppress it and two jets of vomit ejected from her nose.

I'm going to suffocate. She tried to blow her nose clear.

Now I wish I was dead. She cried silently behind the tape.

The car turned onto another rough road and was ascending. Nikki's body rocked with every bump. At last the car stopped. They were on a downward slope. She heard the handbrake ratchet on and a door open and slam.

She held her breath. Is he coming to get me? There's nothing I can do to save myself. I'm just waiting to die. She thought of Lyle. Would he be sad if she died? Would he cry? She doubted it; they hardly knew each other. There hadn't been much chance.

She heard the Inflictor walking around but then there was silence. She waited. Hard objects pressed into her back. The boot was getting hot and it reeked of vomit.

She felt she couldn't breathe properly – how long will the air last in here? This is it. No one's coming to help me. I could identify him – he'll definitely have to kill me, she sobbed.

In the distance another engine rumbled. It was loud and old. The professor *had* come. The old engine juddered and died down. After a moment, a car door opened and then another. She listened.

'I said come alone, old man,' the Inflictor shouted.

'I can't drive – I've had a stroke. I had to hire a chauffeur,' he paused to cough. 'Don't worry, he can't speak English. He doesn't know what's going on. He just drives.'

'Just make him get back in the car. Where's the chuman?' the Inflictor demanded.

'She's here. Show me Nikki first.'

Nikki thought she was going to wet herself. She heard footsteps. The boot sprang open. Fresh, cool air wafted in her face and sunlight blinded her. She blinked. One eyelid was sticky with blood.

A huge silhouette loomed above her. Her hair was grabbed and her head yanked up. There was nothing she could do. She fell back – separated from her wig. Her humiliation complete. For a few seconds, the only sounds were her own squeals of anguish, muffled behind the tape.

'Freak,' growled the Inflictor. That word again. He wrenched her up by the shirt so the professor could see her face.

'My God, Nikki, are you alright?' yelled the professor.

The Inflictor pushed her back into the boot.

'Now get the chuman!'

'Not until Nikki's out of the car.'

Her shirt was grabbed again and her body scraped over the opening of the boot. She flopped to the hard ground like a rag doll. Her wig lay, like a dead thing, beside her.

'Nikki, I'm so sorry.' The professor gave a sob.

Her gaze followed his voice. He looked too frail to help at all. He still had his stick. She struggled to her knees and sat on her heels.

'Shut up and get the chuman,' the Inflictor yelled harshly, and spat.

Nikki knew he was capable of killing. She knew he'd have a gun. Someone was going to get hurt or die here, she just knew it. She blinked away the tears. Then she noticed the chauffeur watching from the professor's front passenger window. He was Chinese and had a chauffeur's hat on. *Lyle?* It was Lyle! Her heart made a little leap in hope – even if he would now see her as a freak.

The professor opened the back door of the Morris and leaned in. Nikki could hear squealing as he struggled to get hold of Cheeka. Almost falling backwards, he lifted her out and set her down but she hid behind his legs. Nikki wanted to call out to her. Tears blurred her vision again and she sniffed, afraid she'd suffocate with a runny nose.

'Put the chuman in my car boot.'

Nikki was seized with anguish. Could the professor part with Cheeka like this?

There was a noise from the slope behind them. The Inflictor spun around, withdrawing his gun as he did. Shots exploded. Cheeka screamed. More shots sounded, pinging off the metal of – a wheelchair! The chair rolled down the hill, shaking, before hitting vegetation and toppling. The Inflictor fired continuously at the top of the slope as if hoping to hit the unseen culprit.

Nathan must have been up there. She yelled for him, but the word couldn't be formed behind the tape.

Lyle sprang from the car and dived at the Inflictor's ankles, knocking him to the ground. On impact the gun jumped from his grasp, landing just out of reach. The Inflictor kicked furiously but Lyle held fast to his legs. The Inflictor stretched towards his gun but Lyle managed to drag him back – just far enough.

'Run, Nikki!' shouted the professor, but she couldn't. She saw her cousin running down the slope and heading straight for the gun, which he kicked across the ground towards the cliff. It bounced off a tree growing at the edge and the Inflictor broke free from Lyle and lunged at Nathan before he could kick the gun again.

'Nathan!' Lyle yelled.

Nathan jumped, swinging his foot around to kick him clean in the chest but a strong hand caught hold of his ankle, toppling him onto his back. Nathan thrust his arm forward and finger-stabbed his assailant's throat. Coughing, the Inflictor grabbed Nathan's arm and smashed his elbow to the ground. Pain electrified his arm. The man made to kick him in the ribs but Lyle swung his arm like an axe and chopped their opponent's neck. The Inflictor, momentarily knocked off balance, yelled in pain and rage. Then he leapt up, spinning around mid air, to plant his heel on Lyle's shoulder.

Lyle staggered backwards, grasping his upper arm.

Nikki winced, imagining his pain. It didn't look like the guys stood a chance against him. She knelt helplessly in the dust, shaking despite the warm sun. Cheeka and the professor had crept towards her. The professor swept up her wig and he and Cheeka dragged her off to the other side of the Morris. The professor tried to remove the tape from her mouth but it was stuck fast.

'Quickly?' he asked.

Nikki nodded. 'Ahh!' And wondered if the skin had come off.

'You alright? Did he hurt you? Your head's bleeding, let me look.' Nikki noticed his voice was shaking.

She blinked, now aware of its throbbing. 'Never mind me, what about them? And where's Einstein?'

'He'd just get himself killed so we left him at your camp.' The professor used a key to saw through the tape that bound her wrists. He tried to rip it off but even his good hand was weak and shaky. Nikki finished the job herself. She quickly arranged her wig and tugged it into place. She turned her eyes to the guys. Could they really overpower a killer? They were already hurt and exhausted but had barely made a mark on him. She frantically picked at a corner of tape on her ankles. They need me.

She'd got enough to unwind. It was all too slow and sticking to her hands. Good enough, and she ran to help them with tape dangling, almost tripping her.

'Nikki, come back!' hissed the professor.

Cheeka shot off ahead of her. In a flash she'd grasped a branch of the cliff edge tree and swung herself up.

The Inflictor's shoe smashed into Lyle's face and he fell sideways, blood spurting from his nose. He didn't get up.

'Lyle!' Nikki yelled.

Nathan swung a kick to the Inflictor's back but he reached back and grabbed Nathan's leg and yanked. Now both boys were on the ground.

The Inflictor staggered towards his gun. He stooped and picked it up, panting like a bull, then looked at Nikki. His left eye had rolled grotesquely upwards, giving him the look of a monster. Behind him and three metres up in a tree, Cheeka was watching. The Inflictor turned, followed Nikki's gaze and whisked up the gun. He was going to kill her! There was a deafening shot.

Nikki's ears rang and she screamed, 'NO!'

Unharmed, Cheeka screeched and leapt to another branch. Nikki sprang to her feet and madly ran at the psycho. All she could think about was stopping him from killing Cheeka. Another shot rang out. Nikki could smell the gunpowder. Mid run she slammed a foot into the side of his knees. He collapsed and she skidded to the ground.

Lying on her back, her muscles froze but she felt her heart would burst. All her consciousness focussed on this last moment of her life and she was barely aware of the others all shouting. The Inflictor stood over her, snarling. The gun was still in his hand. This is the end. One eye stared at her, the other into his head.

This is how I'm going to die.

He slowly raised the weapon to her face.

I could try to kick it from here, but he'd just shoot me as I tried.

In her mind her father's face smiled at her. She saw him clearly this time. He beckoned.

The Inflictor's muscles flexed, ready to fire.

Nikki screamed and shut her eyes. I'm really going to see my dad again, she thought, and her fear ebbed away.

She heard a squeal, and opened her eyes a crack. Cheeka dropped from the tree onto the Inflictor's head. He reeled and swore. Cheeka locked her long fingers together, over his eyes. Blindly, he clawed at her with his free hand.

Nikki leapt up and smashed her fist on the Inflictor's forearm. The gun sprang free. Nathan grabbed it and flung it over the cliff.

The Inflictor hammered Cheeka with both fists. Her feet curved around his neck. He gave a stifled roar.

Nikki and Nathan helped Lyle up, his nose and lip swollen and bleeding. They stood watching Cheeka, helplessly – would she be alright?

The Inflictor spun around and around but she held on tenaciously.

'They're too near the cliff,' Nikki murmured.

Then something the size of a golf ball landed at her feet. She shrieked. 'It's an eyeball.' It rolled to look at her.

The Inflictor lost his footing. He let go of Cheeka. His arms flailed wildly, his fingers splayed like massive claws. He toppled, with Cheeka still on his head, over Lovers' Leap. Nikki screamed. It had all been for nothing – they'd failed to save her. This couldn't be…

The Inflictor roared – the cry of a man falling to certain death.

'Cheeka!' she sobbed. Has she died saving me? She staggered towards the cliff edge, half blinded by tears.

'Let me look first,' yelled Nathan.

Lyle caught her arm and held her back, then his arm moved to her shoulders.

'She *has* to be alright,' she cried. Lyle squeezed her but said nothing. Thoughts crept into her mind – now he knows about me, will he still want to be my friend? How can I think of this now? I must be a terrible person.

They watched Nathan peer over the cliff.

'What's taking him so long?' asked Nikki, wiping away a tear.

Nathan lay on the ground and hung an arm over the cliff. Then Nikki heard Cheeka's excited noises. A moment later, her head appeared above the cliff and Nathan pulled her up.

'You're alright – thank God,' exclaimed Professor Ivanson, limping towards them. 'Thank God, thank God.'

Nikki let the professor hug Cheeka first.

'What about – *him*?' she asked, without looking over.

'See for yourself,' replied Nathan, drying his brow with a corner of his T-shirt.

Tentatively she took a peek. The Inflictor, most definitely alive, was hanging by his hands from one of the tree's major roots poking from the eroded cliff face. The fearsome face gaped in both mouth and empty eye socket. The single eye searched the safety of the cliff edge.

'Let's just leave him there,' said her cousin.

'Cheeka? Where did she go?' The professor whisked his head around.

'Look out,' shouted Nikki.

The Maserati began rolling cliff-wards.

The driver's door was open. Cheeka jumped out.

'Uhh, uhh, uhh!' She jumped up and down.

In slow motion the car approached the cliff. It picked up speed. The front wheels dropped over the edge and it stopped momentarily then leaned over, like a great black rhino taking a drink. Metal creaked ominously. A piece of cliff broke off and slithered down. Stones rumbled over the edge. Then the car tipped almost vertical and suddenly plummeted. Nikki heard it bashing against the cliff on its way down. A couple of seconds later, there was an explosive crash.

They all hurried over to see the upended car, concertinaed with wheels bent outwards and surrounded by sparkling glass.

'He deserved it.' Lyle spat blood.

'But who's going to clean up the mess?' asked Nikki.

'Just enjoy the moment of sweet revenge, Nikki. Look what he did to you,' he responded.

She shook her head and took Cheeka's hand. Secretly, but guiltily, she *did* savour the revenge. She heard the Inflictor's frustrated grunts as he tried to save himself.

'What are we going to do about *him*?' she asked the professor.

Cheeka let go of her and scuttled towards the cliff edge tree.

'No, Cheeka, come back,' cried the professor.

Nikki and the boys rushed after her, arriving just as she disappeared over the edge. Slowly peering over, Nikki found her sitting on the Inflictor's root, gripping it with her bare feet and hands. This close to the sheer drop, Nikki's own hands and feet felt strange. Cheeka's extra weight sent dry soil and stones sprinkling down the cliff face.

'Cheeka, be careful, please climb back up,' she pleaded, feeling ill both from the height and from being so close to that evil man. Cheeka laughed and gave a little jump, sending more stones tumbling. The Inflictor cried out. He swung his legs at the cliff but his feet just slipped off the sheet of rock. Nikki heard wheezing as the professor shuffled up to her. He leaned on his stick and mopped his brow.

'What should we do?' Nathan asked him. 'Do we get help – the police?'

'I suppose we can't just leave him here and not tell anyone,' said Lyle.

Nikki was about to ask the boys to get Cheeka,

when Cheeka reached her hand to the Inflictor's fist.

'No, Cheeka, you mustn't kill him,' she cried, her head spinning.

Cheeka hesitated, her hand hovering just above the Inflictor's. Then she grabbed his wrist and heaved, trying to pull him up.

'Cheeka, be careful, you could fall,' cried Nikki.

* * *

The Inflictor looked into the chuman's eyes. Something flickered there. Something good. Something he lacked. He'd failed – defeated by the creature he'd thought inferior and weak. Its long fingers had cut off his pulse, leaving his hand numb. He felt the burning gaze of hatred from four pairs of human eyes. But the chuman was trying to save him – for what? Prison? No, they wouldn't have him – he'd rather die.

* * *

The Inflictor let go with his other hand and eased her fingers off his wrist. He dropped, silently whooshing through forty metres of sea air. His body struck the dark boulders and crumpled. Nikki felt faint.

'He's dead,' said Lyle.

'No wait,' said Nathan. Nikki chanced a glance and saw the man's legs jerking reflexively in death. Her stomach heaved but was already empty.

'Hey, creep, you forgot your eyeball!' said Nathan, and threw it towards him, hard. The glass eye smashed.

A tongue of water came in and tasted the corpse, then, as if disgusted, the wave recoiled, only to return again with battering force. Finally the sea lifted his body and rhythmically manoeuvred it until it could be claimed in full.

CHAPTER 30

'Nikki,' her mother called upstairs, 'there's a letter for you.'

Nikki threw her legs out of bed. All her mail came via a mobile phone or the Internet, so this must be important. She examined the envelope for clues and recognised Professor Ivanson's unusual spiky "k"s in her name. How was Cheeka now? In her mind she could picture her smiling face and hear her laugh. She tore the envelope with trembling hands. Wait, she told herself, this could be bad news – Cheeka did have something wrong with her kidneys and other things. Heart thudding, the letter drooped in her hand. Then she took a breath and read:

Dear Nikki,

It is with great sadness that I write to tell you of Cheeka's rapid decline in health. I fear she will not be with me for much longer. It would bring us both much comfort if you, Nathan and Lyle would be able to pay us a visit. I have written separately to all your parents, but will understand if you are unable to come. I hope this news hasn't been too distressing for you. If you are able to come, please make it soon. I will have rooms ready for you.

Cheeka often looks at the photos you took last month.

Yours truly,

Henry Ivanson

Two days later, Nikki woke, groggy after a night interrupted by nightmares in which the Inflictor was chasing them again. Daylight flooded the cramped third bedroom of Professor Ivanson's replacement home. She supposed there was no point in him getting a big house again, just for Cheeka and him – and he'd lost all his stuff in the fire anyway.

She checked her watch. Almost seven. Since Nathan's parents had dropped them off quite late the previous night after a long drive, they'd merely peeked into Cheeka's room. She sighed deeply. The room had looked so gloomy and Cheeka was almost invisible in the adult-sized bed. Nikki felt bad that she'd had to shut her door so as not to hear Cheeka's laboured breathing.

What will today be like? Can I face it? Maybe I'll feel stronger with Lyle and Nathan beside me.

She got up and looked out of the little window at the overgrown and ill-kept back garden. A gnarled apple tree and weeping willow shaded a small pond. She was almost surprised to hear the birds singing while Cheeka lay dying so close by. It didn't seem right. She noticed chopped branches piled up at the back of the garden as if for a bonfire. But it was a little early for Guy Fawkes Day.

She heard the clinking of china downstairs and got ready quickly. From the hallway, she spied Lyle and Nathan in the kitchen.

'Amazing – you're up before me,' she said. They were sipping orange juice and nibbling toast, but without their usual enthusiasm. Reading their solemn faces, she stopped in the doorway.

'It's okay,' said Lyle. 'Nothing's happened.' Nikki had never seen him looking sad before. It made him look sensitive, even beautiful, despite being a guy.

'The professor says she's a bit worse this morning,' said Nathan, also looking sad, but not so beautiful with it.

'I really want to see her.' Nikki sat down and took a sip of juice. 'But I'm not sure if I can cope seeing her suffer.'

'She's not just sick. She's dying,' said Lyle.

I guess he's not as sensitive as he looks, Nikki thought, but the truth of his statement cut like a knife.

She heard the creaks of someone coming slowly down the stairs. Her heart quickened. Had Cheeka died already?

'Good morning, Professor,' she said shakily. She didn't just want to say *hello*, but now regretted saying *good* morning. There was nothing good about it.

'Morning, Nikki. I'm so glad that you're all here. Cheeka's expecting you now, if you're ready to see her.'

She got up but felt weak. Her hands trembled as she returned her glass to the table. She followed the professor and could hear Cheeka's rasping breathing from the bottom of the stairs. He stepped into her room and sat on her bed.

'Nikki's here to see you, Cheeka,' he said, stroking her forehead. Then he opened the checked curtains and beckoned. 'I'll leave you for a few minutes, then the boys can see her.'

She approached the bed. A lump formed in her throat. Cheeka's eyes followed her and she managed a weak smile. Her small body lay under a quilt with a cheerful jungle pattern and her head looked comfortable on the pillow. Nikki sat on the edge of the bed and smiled but her eyes misted with tears. She wanted to flee from the room and at the same time to be there, hugging her. She dared to gaze into the face of her little friend. She was deathly pale, but a sparkle in her eyes told Nikki that she was happy to see her. Nikki gently picked up her hand. It was cool and thin.

Does she know she's dying? Her head throbbed and pain knifed either side of her throat with the effort to suppress her emotions. She didn't want Cheeka to see her upset but finally a rogue tear escaped. Cheeka slowly lifted up a finger and wiped it away in mid-trickle. Nikki clenched her teeth in a vain attempt to prevent more and had to look away. Then she spotted one of Cheeka's baskets of twigs and stones against the wall. She reached for it, and began arranging the stones around Cheeka's head, as Cheeka had done for the professor. Her vision swam but she blinked back the tears and tried to continue.

Through her sobs she heard: 'Nikki, Nikki, stop.'

Thinking it was Nathan, she protested. 'But I can make her better. Go away.'

'Nikki.'

She wiped her eyes.

'Cheeka?'

Cheeka's voice was weak but clear. 'Come close.'

'Cheeka?'

'No cry. Come close,' Cheeka slowly lifted both her hands and placed them on Nikki's head. She didn't resist.

She couldn't remember what it felt like to have someone's hand rest on her head like that. Her father used to do it. She hadn't allowed anyone to touch her... her wig. Then Cheeka gently but firmly tugged at the wig and let it slither off. Cheeka placed her hands on Nikki's bare scalp. The hands now felt hot. Cheeka closed her eyes and mumbled words she couldn't make out. Nikki closed her eyes too. She felt a tingling sensation in her scalp, which grew to a vibration. The vibration tickled down her neck to her middle. She was no longer aware of the room or the bed she sat on. Then she felt as if she'd been shot from a cannon. All around her were beautiful stars in the velvet blackness of space. After a moment, the stars turned into fine streaks of light before disappearing. It was as if they had gone beyond the edge of space. What looked like whirling space dust and light gradually condensed into faces. They appeared noble and wise, like the elders in ancient times. Some had heavy brows and eyes that seemed to look straight through her. Then the faces faded into darkness and she felt sucked down into a vortex. Round and round. She felt she would fall off the bed. A whoosh of energy channelled from Cheeka's palms like a river of tiny bubbles.

Then Cheeka said, 'Cheeka finished her work now. No more badness. Only good.'

'But Cheeka, we love you – we want you to stay *with* us.' Nikki, feeling light-headed from the experience, ran her hands over her head and then pulled her wig back into place.

'Time for Cheeka to go.' She weakly squeezed Nikki's hand, as if the last of her strength had gone. 'See me in sun and moon. Hear me in wind and rain. Touch a flower; you touch me.' Cheeka touched her own heart and then Nikki's. 'You in me. Me in you. Friend.'

And with that, Cheeka closed her eyes and exhaled for the last time. Nikki's heart ached. She hung her head and sobbed. Nathan gently took Nikki's elbow and led her away from the bed and hugged her. Lyle put his arms around the two of them and said, 'Group hug.' She realised they must have been in the room all along.

'Did I dream it? Did she really speak?' she asked.

'We heard her too,' whispered Nathan.

Over Lyle's shoulder she saw Henry Ivanson, Cheeka's parental figure, kneel at her bedside and tenderly take her hand. He put it to his face and wept.

'Let's give him some time alone with her,' said Nathan.

Nikki was numb. The next thing she knew she was staring, unseeing, into the shady water of the pond.

'She was very brave,' said Lyle.

'She spoke to me,' Nikki managed. 'She really did talk, I can still hear her voice.'

'We know,' said Nathan, and put his hand on her shoulder.

'She did go peacefully,' said Lyle gently. 'You know, in Chinese, we don't say you die, we say you have a *new body*.'

'A new body, I like that,' said Nikki. She tried to imagine Cheeka well again, jumping up and down, just because of a bus ride. She smiled but spilled fresh silent tears.

The professor, with regained composure, came to join them. He hugged Nikki.

'Cheeka was like a daughter or granddaughter to me. And you've become the same.' He took her elbow and led her back into the kitchen.

'Why did she have to die? We all loved her,' she cried.

'We couldn't save her. No one could have. We could only prolong her life with medication. She was only *really* ill for the last week. It's all over now.'

'When are you going to report – what's their names?' asked Nathan.

'McBraidy and Brindle-Feist. My evidence will go out in the post this morning. The envelope is ready and addressed to the Government Home Office Inspector. He'll contact the police.'

'Will you get into trouble for not reporting it when Cheeka was born?' asked Lyle.

'I hope not. I did what I believed was best, but they may not see it that way. Nathan, will you go to the Post Office to send it special delivery for me? I'll drop you off and then go to buy some food for us to have a small wake at lunchtime. Ring your parents at the B&B and invite them. I know your mother will want to pay her respects.'

'What's going to happen to Cheeka?' asked Nikki quietly.

'We're going to cremate her here.'

'What? In the garden,' gasped Nikki incredulously. 'I don't think I can watch that.'

'Cheeka would want you there. And cremation was

her wish. No one can hurt her now, and no one's going to have her body to study. She wants to go back to the earth.' The professor's voice was quiet and sad. 'And Nikki… I think she was waiting until she saw you again before she could let herself go.'

She stared out the kitchen window into the garden, pondering what the professor had just said. She looked at the pile of wood obviously intended for the cremation. He was so prepared. How could he have done that while she was still up there in her bedroom, *alive*? The professor was speaking, but she barely noticed.

'Nikki?' He touched her arm. 'Nikki, will you help me buy the food? Perhaps Lyle could hold the fort while we're out.

'Yes, alright,' she almost whispered.

Two hours later, Nikki was staring into the flames that licked the sides of the homemade coffin. The daisy chain she'd laid on it wafted in the heat waves. Auntie Lynne stood beside her and they held each other's arms. Nikki glanced over her shoulder at Uncle Pete who was pacing about, well back. He still didn't really trust the professor. Still angry, she supposed. Was that why he was smoking? She'd never seen him do that before.

Lynne patted Nikki's hand and whispered, 'If it wasn't for Cheeka, I might be sitting here in my wheelchair.'

'We only knew Cheeka for a week,' said Nikki.

'But you obviously formed a very close friendship between you,' said her aunt. 'It was just as important to Cheeka as it was to you, Nikki. I only met her once, but she touched me very deeply. I think she communicated to me without words. Because of her, I learned to tap into my own inner resources for healing. You too, Nikki, must learn to do that. You need to learn to forgive yourself. Things will get better for you when you do.'

Her mind went back to that winter afternoon – to the accident. *Please, please can I still go to the party,* she had begged her father. *No, there's black ice on the roads,* he'd told her. But she pestered him until he gave in. Now he was dead because of her.

'It was my fault.'

'You were only eight. He didn't have to take you. It was his decision.' Lynne squeezed her arm.

The professor moved to stand in front of them. None of them had dressed in black, no one wanted to come prepared for a funeral and Nikki doubted Cheeka would have liked black clothes anyway. Einstein, naturally clothed in black, got up from his patch of shade and went to sit beside the professor.

Henry Ivanson began his speech: 'I just want to say a few words about Cheeka and then we could have a two minute silence where we can offer prayers or thanksgiving for her life, in our own private ways.

'We all loved Cheeka. She was very special and unique in so many ways, wasn't she? She touched us all. She brought healing and she brought together the past and the present. Her illness was a dark shadow that lurked in the corner of our lives. It was a lonely life for Cheeka with just Einstein and me as companions, but it had to be like that...'

Nikki shut her eyes and her mind wandered back to

the campsite on Skye where she and Cheeka had sat making daisy chains. Cheeka was frustrated when she broke a daisy but became so happy when she finally put the completed necklace over Nikki's head - such a funny laugh she had...

The professor looked directly at her. 'But despite all the dangers they went through together, Cheeka said that one of her happiest times was with her new friends, Nikki, Nathan and Lyle.' The professor paused and turned to the fire.

'She was my sole companion for the past four years. I will miss her dearly. Goodbye, Cheeka, my dear Cheeka.' And he bowed his head.

During the two minutes silence, Nikki felt her aunt sway and held her tighter. She stole a look at the guys. She knew by the tension in Nathan's jaw that he was fighting his emotions and Lyle shifted from one foot to the other and kicked at some grass, trying to distract himself from the intensity of the scene. Nikki felt numb, beyond tears.

'Shall we go inside for some lunch?' The professor ended the silence.

Nikki took a last look at the burning coffin and followed the others inside.

EPILOGUE

A few months later, Nikki sat in front of her mirror staring at her short brown hair. It was growing darker than the hair she had when she was eight. She glanced through her window to the street. No sign of Lyle yet. Perhaps today she'd let him see her like this. She dabbed a little concealer over a spot. The doorbell rang. Her heart quickened. I'll just go for it. And she jumped down the stairs.

'Hi,' said Lyle. 'You changed your hair. Nice.'

'Thanks. Shall we go? Nathan said to get to his house before five.'

After walking for a few minutes, Nikki ventured, 'Uh – Lyle. What did you think when you found out I didn't have any hair?'

'Oh… I was afraid that creep had ripped your hair off at first. Then I thought he'd killed you and had got an impostor with a long wig on. When I realised it *was* you, I was just relieved that you seemed okay.'

'But didn't you think that I was a freak?'

'Why would I think that?'

'You thought Cheeka was a freak.'

'That's different. She wasn't any proper species. You just lost your hair for a bit. I wore braces last year. Same kinda thing. Now my teeth are fine and your hair's growing back. No big deal.'

'I was afraid of you finding out. People at school give me a hard time.'

He glanced at her, smiling. 'I don't choose my friends based on how much hair they have.'

'I know that *now* – but when we were on Skye, I didn't really know you.'

'Did any doctor tell you why your hair fell out?'

'It happened after my dad died. It was my fault, you see, because I made him drive me somewhere when there was ice on the road.'

'But it's still not your fault,' said Lyle, as they turned into Nathan's street.

'Maybe, maybe not. It's okay, I'm learning to face it now. Nathan's mum told me to forgive myself – so I'm trying,' she paused. 'We kept thinking my hair would grow back, but it didn't – not until Cheeka put her hands on my head. Don't laugh, but I think she helped me get better.'

Lyle shook his head. 'You know, I feel guilty that I didn't appreciate her enough at the time. You were right – she was special.'

In Nathan's living room, Nikki sat with Lyle on the sofa. Her cousin lounged in the armchair with Chieftain stretched along his lap.

Nikki laughed. 'This is the first time that I've ever been keen to see the news.'

'We only gave our testimonies yesterday – do you think they'll say anything about it today?' asked Nathan.

'They didn't even listen to us properly in court,' complained Nikki.

'Yeah,' said Lyle. 'It was all *just answer the question.*'

'They tried to get me to say Cheeka was neglected because she was left alone in the house,' she added.

'At least we got to say how he did a good job of looking after her,' said her cousin, stroking his purring cat.

'Yeah, he taught her sign language, and she had that tree house and all those toys…' she said.

Nathan turned up the sound. 'Mum, it's coming on now.'

'We go live, now, to the Old Bailey where our crime correspondent Nicolas Hutchison is waiting for Professor Ivanson to come out.'

'Good evening. Well, yesterday the three thirteen year olds, who can't be named for legal reasons, testified to the good care that Professor Ivanson gave to the chuman. And here he is now, coming out of the Old Bailey behind me.

'Professor Ivanson, any news, sir?'

'Very good news,' he said. *'I've been completely exonerated, in part due to the testimony of my young friends.'*

Nikki, Lyle and Nathan cheered and gave each other high fives. Chieftain jumped down in alarm.

'That's great. What are your plans now, Professor?'

'To get on with my life in peace.'

'Tell me, was it wrong to create a chuman? She was a lovely creature, so we are told.'

'Yes, she was a wonderful little person, but paradoxically, the world should never see another chuman. Their production is unnatural and would only result in exploitation and cruelty,' he said, and walked away waving.

The screen switched back to the studio where the

newsreader asked the correspondent, *'What can you tell us of the two people behind the creation of the chuman? Is there any progress there?'*

'That's going to take some time. Many months, in fact. It's emerged that Christoff Brindle-Feist has already established chuman cloning laboratories in at least three eastern countries. It is thought that the chumans were to be sold as super-strong soldiers and slaves. But at this juncture it's not clear whether or not other chumans have been successfully produced. An international investigation is now underway. At any rate, Brindle-Feist and McBraidy will be going down for a very long time indeed.'

They all cheered and jumped up. Nikki and Lyle hugged.

Lynne said, 'I'm so proud of you all.'

Nathan switched off the TV. 'What shall we do now?'

'We thought we'd go for a walk in the park,' said Nikki, and they headed for the front door. Nathan stopped to get his trainers.

'Well, actually, Nathan…' began Lyle, taking Nikki's hand.

'Oh…right. I think I'll just stay and mess around on the Playstation. Have a good time.'

'See you later,' said Lyle, as they shut the door and stepped into the sunlight. A gentle breeze caressed Nikki's cheek. She stopped to smell one of Auntie Lynne's pink roses. Cheeka's last words came back to her – *See me in sun and moon. Hear me in wind and rain. Touch a flower; you touch me.*

'I miss Cheeka,' said Nikki, and sighed.